WHERE

LOYALTIES LIE

SHERRYL D. HANCOCK

Published by Vulpine Press in the United Kingdom in 2018

ISBN 978-1-83919-256-2

Cover by Claire Wood

www.vulpine-press.com

To all the amazing staff and agents I worked with at the Department of Justice for many years of my State career, thank you! I learned a lot!

To the pilots I worked with in BNE who taught me the difference between a Queen Air and a Cessna and let me see all the inner workings of their jobs... Thank you! It's an experience I'll never forget and hopefully I got it all right here.

Also in the *MidKnight Blue* series:

CHAPTER 1

San Diego, California, 1993

"Are you ready yet?" Rick asked impatiently. He was standing in the doorway to his and Midnight's bedroom, waiting for her to finish up on the computer. It bothered him a little that she found it necessary to work even at home; their lives had been busy enough lately, and now she was holding them up again.

"Yeah, yeah," Midnight said, holding a delicate hand up. "Is Keyla even ready?" she asked, trying to deflect him from starting an argument she could already feel brewing.

Rick looked over his shoulder. He saw their daughter looking up at him; she was wearing her jacket and the knitted hat she had become very fond of, which his mother had sent from England.

"Yes, Keyla is ready. We're waiting for you," he said. Midnight could hear the "as usual" in his voice. She craned her neck to look at the clock.

"Oh Jesus, Rick, it's only seven o'clock. They don't even get in till eight," she said, exasperated.

"Well, I want to make sure we get there early, just in case, alright?" His voice was taking on an agitated tone. She'd heard more and more of it lately; nothing ever seemed to be okay between them anymore. She hoped that this visit from his sister would improve things.

They'd been married for almost three years now. Their daughter, Mikeyla Marie, who had been born after an extremely difficult labor, was just a little over two years old and very precocious. Mikeyla had received the best features from her parents; she had Rick's deep blue eyes and Midnight's copper-blond hair, as well as her independent attitude. She had started walking at the very early age of eight and a half months, and talking—in complete sentences, no less—at a year and a half. Midnight loved her daughter very much, and found herself constantly trying to do what she felt would be the exact opposite of what her parents would do.

Midnight's mom and dad had essentially abdicated their role as parents when Midnight was young, and had gone back to drinking, drugs, and staying out all hours of the night. It had fallen to Midnight to take care of herself and her younger brother, Thomas. When Thomas had been killed in a gang fight, Jack and Carrie Chevalier had blamed their daughter, since it was her gang Thomas had been fighting alongside that fateful night. Thomas's death had sent Midnight reeling. At the age of eighteen, to her way of thinking, she no longer had a family.

She had continued to have almost no contact with her parents. However, at Rick's insistence that Mikeyla should know both sets of grandparents, she had let him arrange a meeting with the Chevaliers. Jack and Carrie hadn't been overjoyed to hear that they were grandparents, but had, from what Rick said, been enchanted with Mikeyla when he had taken her to see them. Midnight had refused to go, telling Rick that she had no desire to see her parents and that if he wanted them to meet Mikeyla, he was on his own. Rick had been disappointed at her attitude, and had been unable to change her decision in the slightest.

Finally he had given up and taken Mikeyla to meet her grandparents alone. They had been very impressed with Rick and with Mikeyla. They hadn't, to Rick's dismay, asked much after their daughter; when Rick brought up Midnight, they had become rather uncomfortable.

He had seen a picture of Thomas while he was at the house. Thomas had looked a lot like Midnight, and he could see that he would have been a handsome young man. Jack Chevalier had told Rick that they had been very proud of Thomas, that he had done well in school and was generally a good kid, but Midnight... His voice had trailed off as he had shaken his head, as if Midnight were a lost cause. Rick had felt anger rise in him. How could her own parents think so badly of her? And what was this professed pride in Thomas? Midnight had always said that her parents didn't give a shit about her or her brother, and that was why she and subsequently Thomas had ended up in the gang.

Rick had left the Chevalier home with a sense of unreality. He had tried to talk to Midnight about it, but she didn't want to hear anything about her parents. Whenever he tried to bring up going to see them again, she closed down, shaking her head at him as if to say, "You know better."

In Rick's eyes, his wife had changed over the last two years. She had become a very important part of the department since they had gotten married. Suddenly there was an outcry in communities around America for the police to do something about the gangs and the violence. Midnight had been called upon by numerous agencies to conduct training and seminars on the problem, and on the program she had built. She'd been traveling a lot; she'd spent at least a week out of every month traveling to one city or another, speaking on the topic of gangs, or giving briefings to chiefs, sheriffs, and other heads of departments on what their department could do to create their own gang task forces. Now many of the departments were requesting that she return and help them set up the program itself. The chief was more than happy to lend out his star officer to other departments; it was an election year, and all of the publicity on his department being the leader in the war against gangs did nothing but improve his standing in the community. So Rick knew that Midnight would be traveling even more in months to come. He didn't like it—she was never home, and when she was, she was working on some project, like now.

"Night…" he said impatiently, looking at his watch.

"Okay, okay!" she said, standing.

She was wearing black jeans and a black sweater, and Rick had to admit that no matter what problems they had, he still found her incredibly attractive. Having Mikeyla had done nothing to alter her perfect shape; if anything, it had made her curves even more rounded and alluring. She looked up at him now, smiling apologetically.

"I'm sorry," she said softly, "I just gotta get this in tomorrow, and I didn't want to try to do it with Deborah here."

She watched him, hoping that would put an end to the hostility for now. Rick nodded, closing his eyes for a second, knowing that he was overreacting to something that she did all the time—and he knew that getting into a nasty fight about it wasn't going to do either of them any good. He forced himself to let go of his irritation.

"Hey," she said softly, moving to stand in front of him, looking up at him with cat-green eyes.

"What?" he replied, almost petulantly.

"I love you," she said, her eyes searching his.

He grinned, knowing that he was being a shit and that was what she was trying to point out to him. He nodded. "I'm being an asshole, huh?"

Midnight grinned back at him. "Kinda, but I love you anyway."

"Well, thank God for that," he said, pulling her into his arms.

As he held her against him, he remembered their wedding day. Sometimes he wanted to go back and just start again. But he knew they were a long way from that day; he just hoped they hadn't moved too far from those feelings.

"I love you too, baby," he whispered against her hair.

"We'd better get going," she said after a few minutes.

He could hear the reluctance in her voice and he felt buoyed by that. It reminded him that they had a lot to work for in terms of their relationship. They loved each other—about that there was no doubt— but keeping things smooth between two such strong personalities was not an easy thing to do, even with the love that they shared.

They left the house. They still lived in Mission Beach, but they had bought a home in a more affluent neighborhood closer to the ocean.

"I don't want our child to grow up in a neighborhood where she can't play in the front yard," Rick had told Midnight, by way of explaining why he thought a more upscale neighborhood would better suit them.

Midnight had been reluctant to buy in a posh area, not wanting to send the wrong message about them to the gang members she worked with, but Rick had been adamant. "Your job can't dictate everything we do, Midnight," he had said, and she had realized he was right.

"Do you want me to drive?" Midnight asked, eyeing him.

"No, I think I will," Rick said, glancing at her.

"Do you know how to get to the airport?" she asked, her voice skeptical.

"Yeah," Rick said, but a slow grin spread across his face. "Maybe..."

Midnight started to laugh. They were constantly getting lost because Rick refused to take directions from her. She always reminded him that she had grown up in San Diego, and therefore knew it better than her "English transplant". Because of that, he was always determined to find places without her assistance. It had become a constant joke between them.

"If you really want to get there on time..." Midnight said, trailing off as she looked up at the sky unassumingly.

"Oh, shut up, Midnight, and drive!" he said, laughing as he tossed her the keys to his car. He was still driving the Mustang he had bought two and a half years before. Midnight still had her Corvette.

Forty-five minutes later they were waiting at the gate for Deborah's plane to arrive. It was about fifteen minutes late. Rick paced while Midnight leaned against a nearby wall with Mikeyla standing beside her, copying her mother.

When the plane arrived a little while later, Rick stood, looking anxiously for his sister as the passengers started filing through the gate. A bright smile appeared on his face when he saw her. Deborah moved directly to her brother and threw her arms around him.

"Rick! It's so good to see you!" she exclaimed. Stepping back from him, she looked him up and down. "You look great, same as always."

"You too, Deb," Rick said, smiling down at his sister.

His eyes went to her husband, and he inclined his head slightly; he still didn't like the guy. He was almost bowled over by his nieces as they threw themselves into his arms. Deborah moved to Midnight, who stood holding Mikeyla's hand in hers as she watched her husband.

"Midnight," Deborah said, reaching out to embrace her sister-in-law. Midnight hugged her warmly. Deborah stepped back and looked down at her niece. "And this must be little Keyla," she said, smiling her warmest smile at the little girl. She knelt in front of her. "Hello there," she said softly.

Mikeyla looked at the pretty lady in front of her, her blue eyes narrowing just slightly, much like Midnight's did when she was trying to work something out in her mind.

"Who are you?" Mikeyla asked, her voice no-nonsense.

Deborah was taken aback by the child's tone—she sounded so serious. "Well, I'm your aunt."

Mikeyla gave the woman a sidelong glance, which made her look even older. Her eyes were still narrowed. Midnight was laughing by this time, knowing that her daughter was remembering that she and Rick had always told her not to talk to strangers and to be aware of a stranger that was being "too nice."

"Keyla," Midnight said. Her daughter's head snapped up at the sound of her mother's voice. "This is your daddy's sister. It's okay."

Mikeyla looked at the woman kneeling in front of her, her blue eyes searching Deborah's face as if looking for some resemblance to her father. "Hello," she said matter-of-factly after a few moments.

"Midnight, this child is absolutely enchanting, and very well taught, I see," Deborah said, looking up at her sister-in-law, a smile on her face.

"Oh yes, we have her programmed," Midnight said, grinning at her daughter.

"Have who programmed?" Rick asked, walking over to them with a niece to either side. Elizabeth and Susan squealed with delight when they saw Midnight and moved to hug her, careful not to trample the little girl with her.

Midnight hugged both girls, looking up at Rick. "Our daughter," she said. "Liz, Susan, this"—Midnight let her nieces go and lifted Mikeyla up in her arms—"is your cousin, Mikeyla Marie Debenshire."

Liz and Susan stood and looked at the little girl, and Mikeyla examined them from her mother's arms.

"Hello," Susan ventured, putting her hand out to Mikeyla. Mikeyla looked at the girl's outstretched hand, her small brow furrowing, then she looked back at Susan, still frowning.

"Cousin?" Mikeyla asked Midnight, not taking her eyes off Susan.

"Yes, Keyla, Susan and Liz are your daddy's nieces—his sister's daughters, like you're my daughter. Do you understand?" Midnight knew this was a lot even for Mikeyla's quick little mind to digest. Mikeyla shook her head slowly, but obviously getting that these girls were related to her in some way. To Midnight's surprise, she held her arms out to Susan. Susan's eyes widened in surprise too, but she reached up to take her little cousin in her arms. As Midnight, Rick, Deborah, and Deborah's husband, Wilson, watched, Mikeyla laid her head on Susan's shoulder, and with a small hand reached out to touch Liz's hair. She smiled. Susan looked up at Midnight, perplexed, and Midnight smiled.

"She likes you," Midnight said. "She doesn't go to anybody she doesn't know, so she must like you. You too, Liz."

Back at the house, Deborah asked Midnight to give her a tour. They ended up in Midnight and Rick's bedroom.

"Your home is absolutely lovely, Midnight," Deborah proclaimed, sitting down on the bed. Midnight looked at her sophisticated, well-groomed sister-in-law, astounded once again that this woman actually liked her and accepted her. Deborah had been closest to her since Rick and she had been married. They had kept in touch by phone and through the occasional letter, although Midnight had warned Deborah early on that she was not the world's best pen pal.

Deborah looked at Midnight. She thought she had noticed a slight current between her brother and Midnight, and she wanted to ask her about it, but she was concerned with being too nosy. Katherine, Rick's oldest sister, who still didn't approve of Midnight in the slightest and referred to her as "the American," had told her to keep an eye out for any sign that Rick might not be happy. Deborah had no intention of telling Katherine anything, even if Midnight and Rick's marriage wasn't all rosy. Their mother had been concerned too—she had told Deborah that Rick had sounded unhappy the last time he called—but when Anabelle asked her son about his blue mood, he told her nothing was wrong. Anabelle had beseeched Deborah to try and see if there was anything she could do.

Now, Deborah could see all was not rosy on Midnight's end either.

"Midnight," she said quietly, companionably. "Is there something wrong?"

"Wrong?" Midnight echoed, moving to sit in the wing-backed chair across from where Deborah perched on the end of the bed.

"Yes, wrong, between you and Richard?"

Midnight looked at her sister-in-law for a long moment, wondering how she had known, and also wondering if Rick had said something to her. After a long moment, she sighed, leaning back in the chair. "Yes, I guess there is…but I'll be damned if I know what it is," she said, shaking her head slowly.

"What do you mean?" Deborah asked, her concern growing.

"I mean… Things are just real strained right now, and I don't really understand it. Rick and I, we argue, but it's not like fights, you know. It's like disagreements, but they seem to keep us just far enough away from each other to keep us from being totally happy." She looked at Deborah, her face belying her frustration.

"Have you talked to him about it?" Deborah asked.

"No. If I bring it up, he tells me that married people don't always agree on everything, and when I tell him that I think it's not just little disagreements, that there's something else going on underneath, he just shrugs it off and finds a way to change the subject." She shook her head sadly. "I just don't know what it is, Deb. Maybe it's me, maybe…

I don't know." She sounded defeated. It was obvious to Deborah she had been mulling the problem over for a long time, and it distressed her that she hadn't come up with the answer.

"Do you still love him?" Deborah asked gently.

"Oh God, yes," Midnight said, sitting up, her face reflecting surprise at Deborah's question. "I love him just as much as the day we got married, but maybe I just don't show it as much now. I'm not sure… It's really hard to know if you're showing someone you love them enough, you know?" Her eyes begged Deborah to understand. And Deborah thought she did. She was surprised at Midnight's clarity of thought; she seemed to go right to the heart of a situation and analyze it.

"Well, maybe you need to try and talk to him again, and make him listen," Deborah said.

Midnight laughed, looking at Deborah incredulously. "Deborah, I think you know your brother better than that. No one *makes* Richard Joshua Debenshire listen to anything."

"Well, that's true enough," Deborah agreed, grinning at her sister-in-law. "Do you want me to talk to him?" She desperately wanted to help. She thought Midnight and Rick belonged together, and she had always been very happy with her brother's choice of spouse.

Midnight shook her head. "No, I don't want him to think we're ganging up on him or something. Besides, you know how he is about keeping family business, family business."

"But we are family, Midnight," Deborah said.

"Yes, but I meant the Debenshire-Chevalier family," Midnight replied apologetically.

"Yes... I guess that would be the case here, wouldn't it?"

The following morning Midnight got up early to go into the office. She had some things to clear up before taking some time off to spend with Deborah and the girls. She intended to stay in the office for only a couple of hours, but by noon she was fully inundated with requests and problems; Joe was off on a vacation himself, so she was stuck answering everybody's questions and problems.

At one o'clock, Rick came into the office with Deborah, Liz, and Susan in tow. He had stopped by to find out why his wife hadn't come home like she was supposed to, and his sister and nieces had wanted to see where both Rick and Midnight worked. They got a full view. When Rick and the three of them walked off the elevator, the office was in its usual chaos. Rick moved through the group, holding his sister's hand, heading for Midnight's office.

When they got there, Midnight was on the phone, her FORS jacket hung over the back of her chair. When she stood to move to a file cabinet behind her, Rick saw that her gun was in its usual place at the small of her back. He was surprised; usually she put it in her desk drawer when she was in the office. She turned back to her desk, holding the phone and talking all the while.

"No," she was saying, shaking her head, her eyes flashing. "I applied for that warrant myself, and I know that the narrative was sufficient, so don't give me that crap!" She glanced up at Rick, grimacing at having said "crap" in front of his nieces. Both girls just giggled.

Deborah took in the difference in her sister-in-law. It was obvious that she was the boss here, and that she was very capable in that position. As they waited an Asian man came in. He nodded to Rick, then moved to Midnight's desk. He held out a folder to her, and she took it, nodding. She held up a hand to the young man, and he waited obediently.

"Yes, you do that, and get back to me. I want those warrants in my hand by three o'clock. These guys aren't just going to sit around waiting for us to come bust them, you know." She rolled her eyes as the Asian man started to laugh. Midnight listened to the other person again for a moment before hanging up after a short goodbye.

She looked over at Rick apologetically. "I'm sorry, things got a little harried here, with Joe out and everything. That Taos case is trying to go south on us, and Judge Connell is being a pain in the keister again—says our narrative wasn't sufficient. I've been writing them for the old buzzard for almost eight years—I think I should know what he's looking for by now!" She turned to the other man. "Spider, what's up?" she asked.

Deborah watched as her sister-in-law listened to him, nodding. She could see Midnight's mind working over the problem he was explaining.

"Okay, okay," Midnight said finally, holding up her hand. "So what we need here is some assistance from your friends in BNE. Tell them that this guy has weapons and parole violations up the ying-yang, and we don't have the manpower to keep up the twenty-four-hour surveillance. Tell them if they'll assist, we'll split the surveillance time with them. Okay?"

"Yeah, but Midnight… What about the border?" the young man said. "What if they skip?"

"Spider, if they try to skip, you grab 'em, but not until. Otherwise we blow the whole thing. Okay?"

"Okay," he said finally, nodding.

"Okay, now, out with you, and let me know what BNE says, alright?" she said, her smile supportive.

"Yes, boss." Spider gave her a two-fingered salute as he walked out.

"Night," Rick began, irritation in his voice.

"I know!" Midnight retorted, cutting him off. "But I gotta find out about these warrants. If we don't hit these guys they're going to close up shop, and I'm out a hundred and fifty or so man hours without a bust. The chief won't like that much."

"Yeah, and you won't be his golden girl anymore, right?" Rick said derisively.

Midnight looked up at him sharply. "What?"

"Never mind," Rick said, sighing. "So I take it you aren't coming with us?"

Midnight looked at him for a long moment. Deborah could see that she was trying to read his expression, but Rick's face was closed up and cold, which surprised Deborah. Finally, Midnight sighed and shook her head. There was a long silence, and Deborah broke it with an exclamation—she had been looking at the wall behind Midnight, and now, as she walked over to it, she could see all the awards and certificates that her sister-in-law held. Deborah read some of the certificates' narratives about the awards. She was astounded at the amount of them. One had come from the Governor of California; there was another one from the Attorney General of California.

14

Deborah was duly impressed with her sister-in-law, and when she turned to Rick to mention how amazing it was, she noticed the irritated look he was giving her. Deborah was taken aback. Why would he be irritated at her? She suddenly realized that her little brother was actually jealous of his wife's accomplishments. That surprised her; she had always thought her brother above such negative emotions. He had always been so loving, and sweet, but now she saw the jealousy in his eyes.

"We better get going then," Rick said shortly. Deborah nodded, looking over at Midnight. Midnight had not seen Rick's expression; she was staring off into space, a dark look on her face.

"Yes, well…" Deborah said, moving to hug Midnight. Midnight looked up at her sister-in-law and smiled as she reached up to hug her.

"Sorry," Midnight said quietly.

"Don't worry about it, love, you have an important job to do. We'll just see you tonight."

"Thanks," Midnight said. She looked distressed, but Deborah had a feeling it was more to do with Rick's attitude than the loss of a day with her in-laws.

That evening, Midnight listened while her nieces went on about the sites they had seen and the beautiful beaches, and how warm it was. Finally, Deborah told them to hush and eat their dinner of Chinese takeout—"I only order the best for my in-laws!" Midnight had joked, but the humor didn't reach her eyes.

Wilson was off at some business meeting. His bank had an overseas office in San Diego, and he always liked to do business while on vacation—that way he could claim the entire trip as a business expense. Rick thought it was a sleazy way to do things, but he didn't say anything.

"There's a party I'd like to take you both to," Deborah began, watching for Rick's reaction. It bothered her that suddenly she was wary of her brother's mood. He had never been the moody type before—that had always been his best friend Joe's act.

"A party?" Midnight said skeptically.

"Yes, some friends of ours are having a little get-together to welcome us to America. They're English as well, and good friends of our family. The party's tomorrow evening." Deborah kept her tone light, hoping Rick would put the kibosh to the whole idea. She knew how he hated society parties. She was surprised when it was Midnight who objected.

"Well, Deborah..." Midnight began, her tone indicating that she was attempting to be polite. "You see, we're just not the party-going type. I mean... Well, I'm not. I—"

"We could make an exception this time, couldn't we?" Rick said tersely, narrowing his eyes at Midnight just slightly, as if she had been attempting to slight his family in some way. Midnight sighed, looking at him, then at Deborah, who was waiting expectantly to see what would happen. It hadn't been her intention to cause a fight; she thought an evening out would be just the ticket to getting Midnight and Rick back to where they had been before.

"I guess," Midnight said.

"Party?" Mikeyla chimed in, her voice high-pitched as it usually was when she was hoping for something.

"Not for you, little one," Midnight said. She grinned at her daughter, her mood lightening a little. "This is a party for big people. Little people don't have to go."

Although she spoke lightly, Rick caught the word "have" versus the alternative "get" and knew she was irritated at him for committing them to it.

Later that night, as Rick climbed into bed he noted that Midnight's back was to him, a sure sign that she was pissed. He decided to try and smooth things over, knowing how Midnight could be if she was allowed to stew on something for too long. He reached over and pulled her body back against his. He felt her tense and knew she was fighting the urge to pull away from him. It struck him again how different things were between them now. She was much harder to read these days, and he found that he was irritated about that more and more often. He had always known she wasn't an open and gushy sort of person, and that she liked to keep some of her thoughts to herself, but usually she would share those thoughts eventually. Lately, she didn't share anything, and when he asked she'd either shrug or just stay silent. He didn't know what to do. He did know that he hated the idea of her keeping to herself—he knew it was a bad sign for their marriage—but he didn't know how to break the cycle they had started, and he was too caught up in his own feelings lately to even try. He decided to try now.

"Night," he whispered against the nape of her neck. "Baby, what's bothering you?"

Midnight was silent for a few minutes. The silence seemed to stretch out, covering everything else. Rick waited, knowing that she was debating whether or not to tell him, and that asking again would only irritate her or cause her to stay silent.

"Why do we have to go to this party?" she said finally.

"The party?" Rick asked incredulously. "That's what's bothering you?" His tone indicated he thought she was overwrought, nuts.

"Yes," Midnight said, wiggling out of his arms and turning to face him. "Among other things, this party is a bad idea."

"Why?" Rick asked defensively.

"What do you mean, why?" Midnight said, rolling her eyes. "Duh." Her face took on the superior look she wore when she was dealing with a gang member.

"Don't talk to me like that, Midnight," Rick warned heatedly. "I'm not some dumb kid, and yeah, I want to know why this party is such a bad idea."

"I just think it is. Besides, I have better things to do than hang out with a bunch of rich snobs." Midnight sounded angry now too.

"Oh, I see," Rick said, his eyes flashing. "Is that what my family is now? Rich snobs?"

"I didn't say that, but ten bucks says your sister's little get-together is as big as our wedding reception."

"So now you don't like my sister?" Rick knew as he said it that he was being irrational, but he wasn't able to stop the flood of anger that had started between them.

"Oh, Jesus Christ!" Midnight said, sitting up in bed, glaring at him. "I'm not even going to start this shit with you. If you want to go to the fucking party we'll go, alright!" Her body was tense, like it was when she went into a situation she thought might get physical.

Rick sensed it and knew things were getting out of hand. He could feel himself getting even angrier, seeing her reacting to him in that way. He actually wanted to hit her, to show her that he could be tough and dangerous too. The thought struck him like a physical blow. He wanted to hit his wife—what the hell was wrong with him?

He moved to sit with his back to her, keeping his face turned away until he could get his emotions under control. He knew his passion for Midnight had turned almost violent a couple of times, and he was afraid at what would happen if he ever lost control of those feelings. Midnight tended to stir in him a full spectrum of emotions. He loved her very much, but she was as headstrong as he was and they often butted heads. Most of the time one of them would give in, but lately, things had been coming closer and closer to a head. Rick knew he needed to get away, to clear his head, but he also knew nothing made Midnight angrier than to have someone walk out in the middle of an argument.

As Rick warred with his emotions, Midnight watched his back, feeling very angry and emotional and not really sure why. She knew they had just taken another step away from what they had once had, and she didn't know if they would ever find their way back. It frightened her. She had placed all of her trust in this man, all of her love and devotion, and if things didn't work out... she wasn't sure what she would ever depend on again. It was like counting on a life raft when your ship was sinking, and then finding that the raft had a slow leak. Her heart pounded in her chest, her hands clenched and unclenched. She longed to reach out to Rick, she longed to make everything right, but her headstrong stubborn nature said, "Why should I, he started all of this." Midnight stood, and for a few minutes just watched Rick, thinking about what she wanted to say.

Finally, giving in to her wants, she knelt behind him on the bed. She felt him tense as she slid her hands around his torso. She laid her cheek against his bare back and just knelt there, holding him. After a few moments she felt his muscles relax, then his hands slid over hers, his fingers entwining with hers. Glancing up, she noticed that his head was bowed. She felt him caress her wedding ring, the ring that had been his grandmother's, and she knew he was thinking of their wedding day.

"I love you," she whispered, "just as much as I did that day." She heard his sigh, and could almost feel him grin. He had always said it was amazing how well she could read him, like no other woman had ever been able to do. He turned, pulling her around to face him, ending up cradling her in his arms.

"And I love you," he said, his voice soft, his expression tender.

He leaned down and kissed her, his lips moving gently over hers at first, then more passionately. It had been weeks since they had had sex; there had always been something else distracting them. But now there were no more distractions, and they made love, enjoying each other for hours.

Later, as they lay together, both feeling very happy and warm, Midnight rested her head on his chest and traced a lazy pattern over his ever-flat stomach with her fingernails. "Seriously," she said, still husky from their lovemaking, "if you want to go to this party, I'm okay with it. I was just—" His fingers on her lips stilled her voice.

"We'll talk about it in the morning," he said, kissing the top of her head. "I don't want to spoil this feeling now."

"Okay." She was willing to let it go for now, a concession not in her nature.

CHAPTER 2

Joe and Randy Sinclair returned from their vacation two days early, having decided that two weeks in Hawaii was about one week too many and longing for the relative comfort of their own home and their own bed. Plus Joe was getting antsy about being away from the office—and by definition out of touch—for that long. Randy knew that much just by looking at him. Their house, located on a nice quiet street overlooking the ocean, was similar to Joe's first home in La Jolla, but with more updated amenities and a second story where their master suite was located. It was for this room that Joe made a beeline. Randy had expected him to get on the phone the moment they were in his car, but he had contained himself, although she did note that the new state speed limit of sixty-five miles per hour was exceeded by approximately twenty-five miles per hour on a few occasions. She chuckled to herself as Joe, utilizing his long-legged stride to reach the bedroom in the most expedient manner, called over his shoulder in an overly casual tone, "I'll grab the bags in a minute, hon. Don't worry about a thing."

"Right," Randy mumbled good-naturedly. "Sure you will." With that, she proceeded to haul in their luggage. They'd had a good time— she could not say they hadn't. Joe had been his usual attentive self; he had even managed to unwind and enjoy himself for the first week. But after that, it had become increasingly obvious that he couldn't relax for long periods of time, and it became evident to Randy just why Joseph Michael Sinclair hadn't been capable of leading the rich playboy life that he had originally been slated for. She knew that without his work he would be miserable, and that attempting to keep him from doing what he loved would be the most foolish thing a person could do.

Randy admired Joe for the fact that he had so many other options other than to work, and yet he did work, and in a field he loved. "Keeping the world safe for democracy," as he liked to quip. In a way she was jealous—not because the work took him away from her, but because she didn't have something as important to dedicate her time to. She still worked as Joe's secretary, and it just wasn't enough anymore. Recently she had made a decision to change her career. She had been planning to talk to Joe about it while they were on their vacation, but she had the nagging feeling that her plans would not be well received by her husband. What made it even more difficult was that she had already put the plan into motion and, therefore, gone behind his back to do it, and she knew he would not be pleased about that. She needed to tell him, and she was starting to feel very guilty about not doing so, but she knew that she had a right to make her own plans and beat out her own path.

Randy Sinclair, formerly Randy Curtis, had done a lot of growing up in the three years that she and Joe had been married. She had been very shy and quiet when she and Joe got together, and Joe had been everything to her. He had taken her out of her humdrum life and made everything exciting and new. He had taken her places she had only read about in books and taught her things about culture and tradition. Joe had taken her to the opera, he had taken her to see plays, he had taken her shopping in Paris, he had shown her the Louvre and Notre Dame. He had also shown her the fun things. They had gone to

Oktoberfest, they had gone exploring old ruins of castles, he had taken her to what he had called good, old-fashioned taverns in England. He had shown her all of his old haunts from his gang days. In the States they had gone to Disney World and on a tour of historic southern mansions, he had taken her to New York to see a Broadway show, and they had even gone on a two-week trip with some tornado chasers in the Midwest. Randy had seen so many things and enjoyed so much, and she loved Joe for everything he had done for her, but she knew she would never be totally happy unless she had something to do that gave her a sense of accomplishment.

For months she had searched for the right answer. She had talked to Midnight and Joe about what made them tick, why they loved what they did. Joe had a hard time explaining it, but Midnight had been very succinct. She told Randy she loved what she did because she knew without a doubt she was making a difference in the world she lived in. Midnight had said, "When I die, I know that there will be people left here that will say they were glad I was alive, and that if it wasn't for me their lives would have never changed." Randy had seen in Midnight's face that Midnight felt everything she was saying, and Randy knew then that she had to find her niche, her place to make a difference. She had decided that being a police officer was a good place to start, so she had filled out an application for the San Diego Police Department as a cadet.

Later that night, as they lay in bed, Randy couldn't put off the inevitable any longer.

"Joe," she began tentatively.

"What?" Joe asked, his English accent thicker in his drowsy state. He lay on his back with one arm around Randy, the other cushioning his head. He had been half asleep when she spoke. Randy's head rested against his shoulder, her fingers tracing lazy patterns on his bare chest.

"I need to talk to you about something," she said, trying to keep her tone light.

Joe noted the difference in her voice, and he knew something was up. He had known she had wanted to tell him something their whole vacation, but he had let her take her time in coming out with it. He knew she was still shy about telling him some things, and he didn't want to push.

"What is it?" he asked patiently when she remained silent.

"Well, I did something kind of impulsive, and, well, I should have talked to you first, but I didn't, and now…" She trailed off as she shrugged, her motions on his chest a little more agitated.

Joe figured she had bought something expensive, or something like that. He grinned at how paranoid she was. He had never begrudged her a thing, not that she ever bought much with all the money he had. "Okay, so what did you do?" he asked, still grinning. "Should I call in the firing squad?"

"Very funny," she said, knowing that his mood was about to change. "Well, I, uh… I applied for a job," she said in a rush.

"Job?" he said, surprised. "You already have a job, or are you trying to tell me that you don't want to work for me anymore?" His voice still sounded like he was joking; he had no idea what was coming.

"No, it's not that I don't want to work for you. It's just that I need something more, you know, more like a career."

Joe thought about it for a while, remembering that Randy had spent a lot of time a couple of months back talking to Midnight and to him about their jobs and why they liked them. He knew she had been searching for something for herself, and now he was curious about what she had decided.

"Okay, so where did you apply?" he asked.

Her fingers stopped moving, and she looked up at him. "San Diego Police Department," she said quietly.

Joe's brow furrowed. "Babe, I hate to tell you this, but you already work for the San Diego Police Department. I guess it really must be me you don't want to work for." He was trying to adjust to what she was saying, and trying to be fair about it. "I guess I could see how working together and living together would become a little monotonous, and maybe it would be good for you to be a secretary for another unit, get a little more experience or something. Maybe you could work for that new unit in narcotics."

"Joe, I didn't apply as a secretary," Randy said, trying to sound confident.

Joe looked at her for a long moment, totally lost now. "Okay, so what then?"

Randy sat up, looking down at him, feeling the need to move out of their cozy embrace to tell him what she had to. "As a cadet," she said. As the sound of the word "cadet" died in the room, Joe's face went from confusion to understanding, to something very close to anger as he comprehended what she meant.

"A cop?" he asked, deadpan.

Randy nodded.

Joe's mind was working now, turning over what she had said before. "You said you already applied?"

25

"Yes," Randy answered, as if she were a witness on the stand.

"And you didn't bother to tell me about it?" Joe said, barely containing his anger.

"No."

"Why?" His question was so simple, but she didn't have a simple answer for him. She was quiet for a long time, searching for the words to answer him, trying to decide for herself why she hadn't told him.

"I guess because I knew you'd try and stop me," she said finally.

Joe made a sound in the back of his throat, shaking his head. "Damn right I would have."

"So I didn't tell you," Randy stated more confidently.

Joe contemplated her for a moment. He hadn't realized until then how much Randy had grown up in the last three years. He saw the strong set to her jaw and the new air of confidence she was trying so hard to exude. He did not believe that she had done what she said, and he was pretty sure she was just trying to make him aware of her new independent streak, like a child does with a parent. He realized he was going to have to start treating her a little differently now, let her make some of the decisions he had always assumed responsibility for.

"Look," he began, trying not to sound condescending, "if you want a little more independence, that's fine, but I think you went a little far to prove a point, don't you?"

It was Randy's turn to stare at him. He didn't believe her—he really thought she wasn't serious about becoming a cop. In that moment all of her timidity dropped away.

"I am going to become a cop," she said.

Again Joe looked at her, trying to gauge how serious she was. She looked pretty sincere, and he could feel his blood pressure rising again. He shook his head, his face a mask of confidence.

"Yes, I am, Joe. You can't do anything about it," she said.

"Wanna bet?" Joe's voice was like stone now, and she recognized the tone he used when he dealt with gang members who got out of line. Her first reaction was to back off, but her ego got the better of her.

"And what is it you think you can do?" she asked cynically.

Joe raised an eyebrow at her, then his lips twisted in a sardonic grin and again he shook his head as if she were a silly child.

"Oh, I can do lots of things," he said, his emphasis on the word "do." He shrugged. "But I don't have to."

"Why?" Randy said, taking the bait nicely.

Again Joe shrugged as he turned over on his side, facing away from her. "'Cause you'll never make it through the academy," he said, speaking to the wall. He looked over his shoulder at her. "That is, if you even make it through the hiring process."

Randy stared at his back, surprised that he could be so mean. "Oh, I'll make it through," she said simply, then got up and left the room.

Joe lay staring at the wall, a knot in his stomach. She probably would make it through both the hiring process and the academy. And yes, there were lots of things he could do to derail this fledgling career of hers, but he knew that if he did, she'd never forgive him, and he didn't want that. He had hoped that maybe his cold attitude would make her drop the idea; he had hoped that it had just been a passing thought, and maybe it was—maybe she'd change her mind in a week or two. He hoped. The idea of Randy on the street, with all the scum of the earth there to take a shot at her, scared the hell out of him, and he didn't even want to think about what he'd do if something happened to her.

He had lost his parents so long ago, and yet the pain of that loss felt so fresh, it came back in a rush, and he almost gasped at the strength of the emotion. Joe squeezed his eyes shut against the angry, hurt tears that welled up. He clenched his fists and willed the knot in his stomach to unfurl. He lay there for two hours, feeling somewhere between sick and furious, before he finally fell asleep. An hour later, Randy came to bed, crawling in beside him, but for the first time in over three years, not touching him at all.

The next morning, Joe was up and gone before Randy awoke. He headed for the office. He was planning to talk to Midnight, but he realized halfway there that she was supposed to be on vacation, spending time with her in-laws. He figured he'd call her later that day—he needed to talk to her.

****

That morning at the Debenshire breakfast table, Midnight and Rick were obviously in a better mood, albeit very tired. They hadn't fallen asleep until the wee hours of the morning and had gotten up at their usual time of 7:00 a.m. They were sitting at the kitchen table when Mikeyla wandered in. Being her usual quiet self in the morning, Mikeyla rubbed her eyes sleepily as she proceeded to crawl up onto Rick's lap. Without a word Rick handed her a piece of the toast he was eating, and Midnight poured her a small glass of orange juice from the pitcher on the table. Their daughter nibbled at the toast and looked around. This was their usual morning ritual, and Midnight realized how good and comfortable it felt to have it. She considered it their quiet time, before the chaos of the day had a chance to invade.

A half hour later, Susan, Liz, and Deborah came into the kitchen.

"Where's Wilson?" Rick asked, the look in his eyes indicating that he assumed he knew.

"Oh," Deborah said, sighing. "He had another meeting this morning, but he promises that he'll be home tonight to take us to the Thelands."

"Thelands?" Rick said, his eyebrows raised. It was obvious that he knew the name.

"Yes, Richard, the Thelands, and I don't want to hear it. I'm sure Sheila isn't living with them still…" Deborah trailed off as she realized Midnight probably didn't know about Sheila Theland. Midnight confirmed that suspicion in the next moment.

"Who's Sheila?" she asked, her cat-green eyes going from Deborah to Rick. As she realized Sheila must be an old girlfriend or something, she started to grin and wag her finger at Rick.

"Okay, so? She's an ex, you figured me out." Rick was grinning now too.

"Ah," Midnight said, nodding. "Yet another heart broken by Mr. Debenshire. Was this a bad one? Did she, like, try to set fire to your car or something?" Her grin was wider now.

"Shut up, Night," Rick said, trying to stifle his smirk.

"Oh no, Midnight," Deborah said. "Sheila just wanted to marry into the Debenshire family in the worst way, and since Rick was so stubborn she pursued him even harder." She winked at Rick, her smile wide. "Even tricked you into something once, didn't she?"

"Shut up, Deborah." Rick's voice was low, as if he could make it so Midnight hadn't heard that part.

"Tricked you into something?" Midnight asked, her eyes belying the innocence in her voice.

Rick was silent for a minute. "Yes," he said, not looking at Midnight, but giving his sister the evil eye. "You could say that she 'tricked' me into something." His emphasis was on the last word. Midnight knew that meant it was something their daughter and probably neither of Deborah's daughters should hear. That clue explained it all, and Midnight started laughing.

"I don't want to hear it," Rick said, one side of his lips curled sardonically. Finally, stifling her laughter, Midnight got up to offer Deborah and her girls some breakfast. They settled on tea and toast; they were light eaters like Rick.

Midnight took her seat again, which prompted Mikeyla to crawl down from Rick's lap and crawl into her mother's. Rick and Midnight exchanged a smile over their daughter's head. Mikeyla proceeded to put her arms around her mother and lay her little head on her shoulder. Everyone in the room watched, smiling.

"So," Midnight began, breaking the silence. "What's on the agenda for you all today?"

"Well," Deborah said, looking at Rick and her daughters, "to be honest, I'd like to take the day and rest. This time difference is really wearing on me."

"Okay…" Midnight said, her mind working. She wanted to go into the office, to make sure everything was still running smoothly, but she didn't want to start an argument with Rick again so soon. Susan saved her.

"Aunt Midnight," the girl said, her eyes shining with hope, "are you going to work today?"

"Well," Midnight said, her eyes going to Rick, "I do have a couple of things I could clear up. Why?"

Susan was silent for a moment, her thoughts obviously warring with each other. *What's going on here?* Midnight thought. "Well, I just wanted to go with you, to see where you work, you know…"

"You saw where she works yesterday," Rick said, his voice thankfully void of any anger.

"Well, yes," Susan began, obviously trying to decide what to say, "but I didn't really get to see, and if Mum is going to 'rest,' well, I just thought…" Again she trailed off, her eyes silently pleading with Midnight. Midnight knew there was something else going on here, and that it was important to Susan.

"Hey, it's cool. I can just go in for the morning and give Susan a tour, so to speak." Midnight spoke evenly, loath to ruin the morning but wanting to help Susan any way she could.

Rick looked at Midnight, his lips pursed. She knew he wanted to tell her no, she knew he wanted to argue, but she could see that he didn't want to start a fight again either—it was too soon. Finally he nodded, and Susan broke into a brilliant smile.

"When will we leave?" Susan asked, a little too excitedly.

"How about in an hour?" Midnight said, looking at her watch.

"I'll be ready." Susan promptly excused herself from the table.

Forty-five minutes later, Midnight was standing in front of her vanity mirror, brushing her long copper-blond hair. Rick moved behind her, his hands on her waist, his eyes watching hers in the mirror. He felt the slight tensing of her muscles and knew she was worried that he wanted to fight. His eyes reflected sadness.

"How did we get here?" he said softly.

Midnight watched him. "I don't know," she said matter-of-factly. "But we're here, aren't we?"

"Midnight..." Rick began mournfully. He turned her to face him, his deep blue eyes searching hers. "I love you so much, sometimes it scares the hell out of me, because I want all of you. I don't want to share you with work, I don't want to share you with anyone, not even yourself—but I can't have that, can I?"

Midnight stared at him for a long time. He had never said this in quite this way before. Finally, she shook her head, slowly, almost sadly. "No, you can't... but it didn't use to be this way," she said quietly.

"Yes, it was," Rick replied. "I just hid it better then." His voice held a note of resolve. "I don't know, Night. I guess it's because I've never felt this way about anyone, and I'm always so afraid that we'll lose it, ya know?"

"Yeah, I know," Midnight said. "But aren't we losing it anyway? I mean, aren't we losing us?" There was no accusal in her question, only sadness. She knew her headstrong ways were partially to blame here too.

"Yeah, maybe, but I don't know what to do."

"I don't either, but we've got to try. There's too much here at stake."

"Yeah." Rick hugged her close to him, and they just stood that way for a long time. Susan appeared in the doorway a few minutes later, and they moved apart. Midnight moved to grab her jacket off of the wing-backed chair and walked toward the door. Rick stared after her, long after he heard the front door close.

In the car on the way to the office, Susan took note of her aunt's attire. Midnight wore black leggings, black boots, a sapphire-blue cotton button-up shirt, and her FORS jacket. Susan silently wished for a body like her aunt's. She thought Midnight was the most beautiful woman she'd ever seen and wanted to be just like her. She had always thought her Uncle Rick was handsome and knew that he had always had girlfriends, lots of them. Susan admired Midnight for the simple fact that she had managed to catch Uncle Rick and make him fall in love with her, but she also admired her for something else. Gathering her courage, she decided to ask her aunt the question she had been longing to.

"Aunt Midnight?" she said tentatively.

"Hmm?" Midnight was still thinking about her and Rick's exchange.

"Can I ask you a question?"

"Sure, what is it?"

"Even if it's personal?"

"Okay…" Midnight replied, wondering what Susan was getting at.

"Did you ever, I mean, is it true, um…" Susan hesitated again, and Midnight felt impatience simmering.

"Susan, what is it? What do you want to know?"

"Well, I wondered if it was true, that you and Joe Sinclair were, well, together…" The whole thing came out in a rush, and then Susan looked very embarrassed as Midnight started to grin, shaking her head in disbelief. *All this for that?* she thought.

"And where did you hear that?" Midnight asked companionably, making Susan relax a little.

"I overheard my aunts and my mum talking about it."

"I see." Midnight smiled, remembering the scene at Harrods almost three years ago now, when Rick's sister Katherine had verbally attacked her about being with Joe.

For a few moments, the only sound in the car was the radio playing Janet Jackson's "Escapade."

"Yes," Midnight said finally. "It's true, Joe and I were together."

"Really?" Susan's eyes widened. She had been wondering for a long time now. She didn't know if her Aunt Katherine had just been being mean—Katherine didn't like Midnight at all.

Midnight laughed. "Yes, really! Did you think it wasn't true?"

"Well, I didn't know. It was Aunt Katherine, after all…" Again Susan's voice trailed off, as she realized she probably shouldn't be speaking ill of her own aunt.

"Yes, I understand that." Midnight grinned.

Susan was silent for a few minutes, digesting the fact that Midnight and Joe had been together.

"How long?" she said finally.

"How long were we together? Oh, I'd say about two years, off and on."

"Wow! Really!"

Again Midnight was laughing. "Yes, really!"

"So you two were, um, close." Her emphasis on "close" indicated exactly what she meant.

"You mean did we sleep together?"

Susan turned a couple shades of red, then blurted out, "Yes."

Midnight hesitated this time. She didn't know why Susan was asking all of this; she suspected she had a crush on Joe and wanted to talk to someone about it, but Midnight wasn't sure she should be the one to do that—it seemed like a job for Deborah. But she knew it could be hard for a girl to get her questions answered by her own mother, and if she didn't get the answers there, she might look for them somewhere else—and who knew how informed that source would be.

"Yes," Midnight began carefully, "we did sleep together." She left the conversation open for Susan to ask other questions. She could see the girl wanted to ask more, and she hoped that by staying silent she was encouraging her to do just that.

"Did you love him?" Susan asked, obviously feeling more comfortable.

"Yes, I did love him. I still do, just not the way I love your uncle."

"There's different kinds of love? I mean, different kinds like when you sleep with someone?"

Midnight smiled, seeing Susan's conflict. She wanted to know how Midnight could love Joe enough to sleep with him, and then love

Rick the same way and sleep with him. *I don't remember having these problems when I was her age*, she thought.

"Yes, there are different kinds of love. It's hard to explain, but I loved Joe because we were the very best of friends and we needed each other."

"Needed each other?" Susan was still confused.

"Yes, this was in the early days of FORS and things were very dangerous for both of us, and we knew that one of us may not be there the next day. We were very protective of each other, because we both had lost so much, and it just translated into a very close relationship that turned into love, and became making love. Does that make any sense?"

Susan thought about it for a while, then nodded. "But how is your love for Uncle Rick different?"

Midnight had to think long and hard about this one. It had been hard to work that out for herself, let alone know how to explain it to someone else. "Well, your uncle and I have a totally different relationship. We love each other because we're alike and different too. You see, with Joe, I loved him because he was my friend and I knew that he'd always be my friend. With Rick, it's like a friendship, but much, much more. We're very, um…passionate for each other. It's much more than just a comfortable friendship—we're willing to change for each other, to make the relationship grow. With Joe, it was 'Take me as I am, 'cause that's all you're gonna get.' Your Uncle Rick and I made a real commitment to each other, by getting married."

"So you wouldn't have married Joe?"

"At one point I might have, if only to have something to hold on to. But in the end, no, I wouldn't have, because he and I were just too wrong for each other. Joe needed something I couldn't and wouldn't give him."

"What was that?" Susan sounded almost awestruck that someone would not want to marry Joe Sinclair.

"Joe has a real need to be needed. He needs to take care of someone and nurture them, and I'm just too independent for that. Your Uncle Rick understands that, and loves me anyway." As she said the words, Midnight thought about what Rick had said this morning—"I want all of you." So did that mean he wanted her to be dependent on him? Midnight wasn't sure, and that scared her more than anything.

They continued the ride into the office in silence, each of them thinking their own thoughts. Midnight was sure she hadn't heard the end of this, and she was actually glad that Susan trusted her enough to talk to her about such things. She was also glad that she could be there for her niece; she missed having a younger person look up to her and need her guidance.

Midnight introduced Susan to members of FORS as they went into her office. Susan acted much as her mother had the day before, walking over to Midnight's wall filled with awards and certificates and reading each and every one.

"Aunt Midnight," she said after a few minutes.

"Hmm?" Midnight didn't look up from the report she was reading.

"What's it like, being so important?"

"Important?" Midnight was surprised by the word. She had never thought of herself as important.

"Yes," Susan said, moving to sit in the chair across from Midnight's desk, her face earnest. "I mean, if you have been recognized by so many people, then you're important, right?"

Midnight grinned. "I guess, but just try reminding those people of that when it comes time to make a new budget, then suddenly you couldn't possibly need anything, no matter how important they think you are."

"So you mean, they didn't really mean what they said on those awards?" Susan asked, perplexed.

Midnight looked thoughtful for a moment. *Good question*, she thought. "Well, I think they mean it," she said. "It's just that money's tight right now, and I guess they feel like as long as they get the level of service they've always gotten, then everything's alright. They don't really realize that my expenses for my unit have gone up and my members expect more for salaries now than they did ten years ago, and I'm having to compete with the money they would be making if they stayed on the street and continued committing crimes. And believe me, there's not much of a comparison there."

Susan thought about that for a while. "So your employees really were gang members?"

Midnight nodded.

"And they really committed crimes? You mean stealing and the like?"

"Stealing, selling drugs, prostitution, all the good stuff, yeah," Midnight replied. Susan's eyes widened, as if she had just realized that the people she had been meeting all morning were criminals. Suddenly she looked worried.

"Have any of them ever killed anyone? I mean, as a gang member."

Midnight grinned at that, then shook her head. "No, if they'd killed someone they'd be in jail."

"Have you ever killed anyone?" Susan asked, her youth making her seem so innocent as she asked such a loaded question.

"Yes, I have," Midnight said, and continued quickly when Susan's eyes became as wide as saucers. "But only in the line of duty—only while I've had the law on my side."

"Oh," Susan said, then was silent for a moment. "Has Joe killed anyone?" This time she waited expectantly for an answer. Midnight wasn't sure what Susan wanted to hear, but before she could answer another voice spoke for her.

"Yes, and he's considering killing one more."

Susan and Midnight looked up to see Joe standing in the doorway. He looked tired and irritated. He was wearing jeans and a blue shirt with his black FORS jacket; he still wore his hair shaggy and long, and his light blue eyes burned with anger. Midnight had to admit he looked good in spite of his apparent mood. Susan just stared at him; the girl definitely had a crush.

"Joe," Midnight said, smiling and wagging a finger at him. "That was a short two-week vacation." She pointedly looked at her calendar. "About two days short."

"Shut up," Joe said, grinning in spite of himself. He went to the chair next to Susan, ruffling her hair as he sat. "How's it going, young lady?"

Susan didn't reply at first; she was too busy being tongue-tied. "Okay," she said finally.

Joe looked at the girl for a moment, wondering why she was staring at him like that, but then mentally shrugged it off—it must be some adolescent thing.

"So," Midnight said, breaking the silence. "Who are you going to kill, and why?"

Joe glanced at her, trying to decide if he should ask her about Randy or accuse her. "Did you know about this little career change Randy is planning?"

Midnight looked blank.

"Obviously not," Joe said.

"So, what is this new career?" Midnight asked.

"She wants to be a cop." Joe expected Midnight to be shocked, but when she nodded, as if expecting there to be more to the story, he was the one who was surprised. "Night!" he said, stressed. "How can you just sit there and nod?"

"Joe," Midnight said, mimicking his alarm and grinning. "What's wrong with that? In case you didn't realize it, we happen to be cops."

"And in case you don't realize it, we're talking about Randy here, not you or me. Little Randy... Ya know?" He was talking to her as if she had some kind of head trauma and she didn't remember who Randy was.

"Yes." Midnight smiled. "My dear Englishman, I do remember Randy, and as I recall she is an adult and has the right to make her own decisions about her career."

"Like hell she does!" Joe snorted indignantly.

Midnight leaned forward. Making a fist, she knocked on Joe's forehead pointedly; Susan had to stifle a giggle. "Hello?" Midnight called. "Earth to Sinclair, come in, Sinclair. This is the twentieth century, you know. Women's lib and all that crap. You can't tell her what to do, Joe."

Joe narrowed his eyes at her. "Why not?" he asked belligerently, like a schoolboy denied a field trip.

Midnight couldn't help but smile at her partner of over ten years. "Because, honey," she said, overly sweetly, "women have rights too, and you men are just going to have to remember that, or we'll have to put a nice bat over your heads."

At that, Susan did giggle.

"What's so funny?" Joe asked, turning to her, grinning broadly. Susan immediately covered her mouth, her eyes wide as she shook her head. "Nothing," she muttered, but her smile was evident.

"I see," Joe said, still grinning. He turned back to Midnight. "So what, oh lady of the downtrodden, am I supposed to do?"

"You," Midnight said, pointing at him, "are supposed to be supporting and loving—and try to curb your attitude."

Joe shook his head, his expression serious now. "I don't think I can, Night. I can't let her do this. If something happened to her..." He didn't need to explain to Midnight—she'd been there before too.

"Joe, come on. Realistically, what are the odds of something happening to her? And even if the odds were greater, there's nothing you can do. You can't protect her all her life, and if you keep trying, she's going to resent you for it. Is that what you want?"

Joe looked at his partner for a long time, then finally blew his breath out in a sigh and shook his head. "No."

"Alright then. Besides, you never know, maybe she won't like it, maybe this is just a phase and she'll decide on something else. But I guarantee you one thing." She paused, looking at him pointedly. "The more noise you make about it, the less she'll listen."

"Great," Joe said simply. But he knew Midnight was right, and he knew he didn't really have any options at this point. He decided he wouldn't try to dissuade Randy from her career path, but he couldn't be totally supportive either. It just went against everything he felt.

CHAPTER 3

Susan and Midnight arrived home a little after one o'clock. Midnight spent the rest of the afternoon playing with Mikeyla and just relaxing. Relaxation was difficult for Midnight Chevalier-Debenshire to achieve; her mind was turning constantly with things she needed to do and people she needed to talk to. In the office that morning she had received a request from the Seattle Police Department to come and speak about FORS. They wanted her there the following week, and she knew that was going to cause another fight between her and Rick.

At a little before five, Midnight went to take a shower and get ready for the party. She was already dreading the boring evening ahead; she knew how these things went. She'd have to deal with a bunch of stuff-shirt, high-class, over-educated rich people, and she'd hate it. Midnight considered begging off, claiming she had a headache, but decided it wasn't worth the effort to argue with Rick. After all, it was just one evening, right?

As she stood looking in the mirror, putting on the makeup she rarely used, Rick walked into their bathroom. He looked very handsome in a navy blue suit; the color almost matched his eyes. He wore a crisp white shirt and a burgundy-and-navy tie.

"Wow!" Midnight said, turning to look at him. Rick grinned. "New suit?" she asked, though she knew it was—he didn't own many suits.

"Yeah, I didn't really have anything to wear to this thing tonight, and Deb said a tux would be a little much."

"I see." Midnight put her arms around his neck, looking up into his eyes. His hands moved to untie her bathrobe, and then to her waist, touching bare skin. He pulled her flush with his body, his lips moving to hers. Midnight entwined her hands in his hair, still worn long and shaggy.

"What time are we supposed to leave?" she asked

"Six thirty."

"Oops! I've only got fifteen minutes left to get ready, don't want to hold everyone up…" She reached up to kiss him again. "Unless you want to stay here instead…"

"Oh no, we're going, but after the party—that's another matter altogether." His grin was wide.

"I see," Midnight said. "Have your cake and eat it too, huh?"

Rick nodded, smiling. He turned and left the bathroom, leaving her to finish getting ready. Fifteen minutes later she came out of their room wearing a burgundy silk dress, her copper-colored mane pulled back with a pearl hair clip. Rick was once again taken aback by how beautiful his wife could be when she dressed up, even more so than she always was. He felt puffed up with pride.

"Oh, Midnight," Deborah exclaimed. "What a beautiful dress! You look wonderful! Now I feel absolutely dowdy."

"Oh, stop," Midnight said, smiling. "You couldn't look dowdy if you tried." Her words were sincere. Deborah was wearing a very elegant cream Chanel suit, and her hair, nails, and makeup were absolutely flawless, as always.

44

"Are we ready?" Wilson asked, joining them. Midnight realized this was just about the first time she had seen him since they had arrived in California. Once again she was surprised at how fair-skinned he was; he was so different from Rick. Wilson had cultivated the strictly clean-cut, clean-shaven, stoic banker look. His hair was a lighter shade than the regular brown of his eyes. His suit was a classic dark gray, and although very expensively cut, it didn't seem to look quite as good on him as it should have. Wilson was thin in a non-athletic way, the opposite of Rick's trim, fit, swimmer's body. No matter how Midnight looked at Wilson, she could not see anything that would be attractive to a woman as quiet and caring as Deborah; she just didn't know what Deborah saw in him.

The babysitter arrived a few minutes later. As they were leaving, Deborah told Midnight they should consider getting an au pair.

"A what?" Midnight asked.

"An au pair. It's a girl that lives with you who acts as a nanny and does some light housework as well. We had one when the girls were younger—they're great. I can give you the name of a good agency here in California if you'd like."

"It's something to think about," Rick said, watching Midnight closely. He knew how she hated anything that seem too high class.

"Maybe," Midnight said simply.

Rick drove to the address Deborah gave him. Midnight noted that the house they pulled up in front of was only a couple miles away from Joe's. *Good, if I need to escape I'll know where to go*, she thought. The house was big, a modern style with large panels of glass in front. Once inside, Midnight noticed that the decor tended toward bright, bold colors. She hated it on sight. She told herself she was being too negative and that thinking this way wouldn't help the night go any quicker, so she tried to look for something positive and nice about the house.

When she met the Thelands, she realized she was indeed a Christian in the lion's den. David Theland was very boorish, with his starched white shirt and black suit. His nails were buffed to a high sheen—and his mannerisms seemed to be too. He spoke to Rick and Deborah first, having known them since childhood.

"Richard, Deborah! How ever are the two of you? Angela is here somewhere, and she will be so happy you could join us." His voice was pitch perfect, somewhere between bored and droll. His English accent was still there, but much less pronounced than Rick's. Midnight was shocked when Rick's whole appearance seemed to change as he spoke with the older man, showing a side of him she had never seen before. He was proper and cool, his tone of voice was different, and when he introduced her to Mr. Theland he seemed to have a hard time with her name, as if it had suddenly become foreign to him. David Theland's ice-blue eyes came to rest on her, and seemed to widen a little in surprise. Midnight felt herself being appraised, like a head of cattle. She knew she should extend her hand to Mr. Theland as Deborah had done, but somehow she just couldn't do it. Something told her this man wouldn't kiss the back of her hand gallantly as he had Deborah's. So she merely nodded to him, her eyes never wavering from his, which seemed to take him back a bit.

"Miss," he said. He narrowed his eyes at her just slightly, thinking her a rude American, and turned his gaze to Wilson. "Wilson, my boy, how are things in the financial circle?"

Midnight felt Rick's hand on her arm, and she moved away with him. He led her over to a staircase of chrome and glass and turned her to face him.

"What was that all about?" he whispered harshly.

"Excuse me?" Midnight said, surprised that he seemed to be attacking her.

"You could have at least been polite."

"Polite? Gee, I'm sorry if I don't know all the English etiquette."

"You seemed to do fine at our wedding," Rick retorted, still whispering.

"Yeah, well at our wedding you seemed to have no problem pronouncing my first name either," Midnight said calmly.

"What's that supposed to mean?"

Midnight stared at him in disbelief. Did he really not realize he was acting totally out of character? "Never mind," she said finally, sighing. "I don't want to get into a big nasty fight right off the bat. I'm sorry I didn't do whatever I was supposed to, okay?"

"Fine," Rick said, and started walking away. Midnight trailed after him, feeling very out of place and angry that she did. Walking to the "sitting room," she stood at the threshold and looked around. The room had cathedral, stained-glass ceilings, the setting sun making the colors dance. Finally, she had found something positive about the house. When she looked around at the people in the room, she saw Rick talking to a woman about her height with short dark hair and very pale skin. *She's got to be English*, Midnight thought, then chided her negative attitude again. She strolled over toward Rick, though he didn't seem to realize she was there. He was very animated as he talked with the woman. Midnight stood behind and off to the right of them, feeling once again totally out of place. Finally, Rick turned and looked at her.

"Midnight," he said, reaching out to her. Midnight looked at his hand, then at him, and stepped forward. She didn't take his hand, and he dropped it, practically glowering at her. He looked at the woman he had been talking to, and she raised an eyebrow at him as if to say, "Her?" Rick smiled and shrugged, then said, "Sheila, this is Midnight. Midnight, meet Sheila."

Sheila looked at Midnight and Midnight stared back.

"Hello," Sheila said finally. "Richard has told me about you and your daughter. She sounds lovely." Her accent was as polished and upper crust as her father's, and Midnight had to hold down the urge to laugh.

She felt like she was in some awful B movie, where the little pauper girl gets to go to the palace and meet the king and queen. *God, I don't want to be here*, she thought. But she smiled wanly at the other woman. She heard a bell tinkling in the foyer, and an English voice rang out, announcing that dinner was served. Again Midnight had to hold back her urge to laugh; this was absolutely unreal. She looked at Rick and saw that he and Sheila were talking again, so she went toward the dining room to find Deborah. She found her talking to Wilson and a dark-haired older woman that Midnight thought had to be Mrs. Theland. Deborah introduced her.

"Angela, this is Midnight, Richard's wife," she said, putting her hand companionably on Midnight's arm.

"Midnight?" Angela Theland repeated. Midnight was surprised that her voice was devoid of any accent whatsoever. "What an interesting name." Midnight didn't hear any insult in the comment, but she wasn't sure that rich people just didn't cover rudeness better than others.

She seemed very nice, but Midnight didn't really bother to think about it much, knowing that odds were good she'd never see the woman again. Mrs. Theland showed Midnight where she was to be seated; she was not pleased to note that she was only five chairs away from ol' stuff-shirt Theland. She could already hear him regaling his subjects with some tale. As she tuned in to the conversation, on the off chance that it might be something interesting, she heard Theland say, "Oh, yes, something else my tax dollars will have to pay for, so they'll raise my bloody taxes again—for what? So some bureaucrat can save some gang member or help some homeless kids. What do they really do anyway? It has got to cost less to allow these misguided children their freedoms than it does to try and stop them!" His voice was indignant and infuriating at the same time. Midnight tried for approximately a fraction of a second to keep her mouth shut, but she just couldn't manage it. She began to shake her head, as if the man were a schoolchild to be scolded. David Theland didn't take kindly to that kind of mockery. "You have a different opinion, young lady?" he asked, raising a cynical brow.

"As a matter of fact, Mr. Theland, I do," Midnight said, taking on an instructional tone. "The approximate cost of gang violence is five hundred and forty million dollars in Los Angeles, according to the LAPD, so yes, they do cost us all money, and no, it wouldn't be cheaper to allow them free rein, sir. These aren't misguided children. Some of them are cold-blooded killers who'll blow you away for ten bucks to buy some crack."

"And how is it you know all of this?" Theland said rudely.

"I'm a police officer, that's how I know, and I work with these kids every day. I know what they're capable of, and they're out there right now building their little drug empires, and unless we stop them, they'll just take over." Midnight spoke with the conviction of fifteen years of struggle, but Theland didn't hear any of it. He was too busy being a pompous ass.

"Well, Officer... Debenshire, is—"

"That's Lieutenant Chevalier," Midnight said, emphasizing her rank.

"Ah, yes," Theland said, not missing a beat. "Well, Lieutenant, maybe then you can explain to me why we don't just legalize these drugs that you police persons claim are so detrimental to society. It seems to me that narcotics are a victimless crime, and the police should just keep their noses out of our business."

The people at the table were all staring now, nodding their heads in agreement with David Theland's statement. Some were looking at Midnight for her response.

Midnight grinned sardonically. *These liberals*, she thought. "Victimless crime?" she said sarcastically. "Oh yes, drugs are a victimless crime. Try telling that to the crack babies that are addicted at the moment of birth, or try telling the women and children who are victims of abuse due to the effects of drugs." Midnight saw that Rick had come into the room and was glowering at her. She knew he was going to be all-time pissed off at her for this, but she wasn't about to stop now and let that pumped-up peacock win the battle. Still standing, she motioned to take in the whole table of people. "What about all the people killed every year by addicts looking to make a score? These misguided children, as you call them, who'll steal a little old lady's false teeth if they think they can hawk them for enough to score a dime bag?"

She moved to stand next to Mrs. Theland, who was watching the exchange as avidly as the rest of the party. "And would you still say that drugs are a victimless crime, Mr. Theland, if your wife or your daughter was raped and murdered by some hype who had just shot up and gotten rid of all those inhibitions that us normal law-abiding citizens have? Would drugs be a victimless crime then?" She looked at the people standing and sitting around the table, then back at Mr. Theland. "And for your information, Mr. Theland, you pay us those hard-earned tax dollars to protect you." She pursed her lips and tilted her head at him, as if sizing him up. "Even if it means protecting you from yourselves." The whole room started talking, and Midnight knew she had made an impression. She also knew she'd never be invited back to the Thelands' again, and boy, wasn't that the icing on the cake! Rick was standing next to her now—he grabbed her arm with a grip of steel.

"What in the hell are you doing?" he whispered harshly.

Midnight pulled her arm out of his grasp, eyeing him contemptuously for not supporting her, and said, "Leaving."

She turned and walked out of the room. Rick followed her, but then she heard a female voice with an English accent that she knew wasn't Deborah's call him back. Midnight couldn't believe it—he actually stopped and turned around. *Son of a bitch*, she thought. She couldn't believe he was actually going to let her leave. *He probably figures I'll calm down and come crawling back.* Midnight lifted an eyebrow in reflection. *Then he doesn't know me very well.*

She got all the way to the front door before she realized Rick had the keys to the car.

"Shit," Midnight said out loud, shocking the stuffy butler standing near the door. She gave him a somewhat acerbic smile, as if the word had slipped out, then proceeded to cuss her way out the front door and down the steps. Thankfully she had kept her purse with her, and in the tiny little useless thing she had managed to stuff her cell phone. Thanking her maker, she pulled it out and dialed Joe's number. After the third ring Joe answered, his voice groggy from sleep.

"Hello?"

"Joe, it's me."

"Who else would it be?" he asked, with his usual humor.

"Look, I need you, now."

"I could say—"

Midnight cut him off. "Don't go there."

Joe chuckled, then sighed. "Where and why? Do I get a why this time?"

"Ten fifty-five Palace Place, and I'll give you the why when you get here. Just hurry up." Midnight was starting to feel the chill of the ocean air; she had left her coat with the butler. She sighed. *I'm not even going to try for it.* She sat down on the low marble fence and waited for Joe, like a sad, dejected debutante with an attitude. She hoped silently that Rick would come looking for her, but he never did, and that really irritated her. By the time Joe arrived she had knotted herself up pretty good; she was almost sputtering.

Joe took note of her condition and meekly asked if she wanted him to stop at a local bar first, before taking her home.

"No," she said sullenly, "just take me home."

"Bad party?" he asked, lightening his tone. "No good games?"

"Oh yeah, great games!" Midnight exclaimed, blowing her breath out in a whoosh. "I think they called it 'Let's Spin Up the Cop and See if She'll Blow.'"

"Oops," Joe said, starting to get the picture. "And did she?" He knew the answer even as he asked it.

"Duh," Midnight said simply. She rested her head back against the seat. "Why did I even agree to go to this thing? I knew it was a bad idea, but Rick said we should and I didn't want to fight..." She trailed off dejectedly, knowing they were going to fight now anyway.

"Rick's not usually into those gigs anyway—what's with him?" Joe asked, remembering all the times he and Rick had been forced to go to debutante parties, how they both had bitched the whole time and shot out of them like rockets as soon as it was socially acceptable to do so.

Midnight scrubbed at her face. "I don't know," she said, her voice muted by her hands. Then she looked at Joe. "Deborah wanted us to go. Maybe it was because of her—maybe he thought it would be nice for her, and maybe that's why I agreed to it. I didn't want to get into another fight about it, because that seems to be my whole life with him lately." Again she leaned back against the seat. "I have such a headache."

"You two are having problems too?" Joe asked, surprised. He knew Midnight had been very busy as of late, but he didn't know it had started causing them marital trouble. "What's goin' on?"

Midnight shook her head. "I don't know, really. It just seems like lately Rick's been all over me about work, that I work too much and I'm not home with Mikeyla, and all that crap. I don't know what to do.

I mean, you know how much momentum FORS has been gaining, and if I try to put the brakes on now, the impact could be disastrous. I certainly don't want all these agencies starting their own units not knowing all the drawbacks and provisions that need to be made. I mean, if they didn't check a member's background just right, if they had just one infiltration, recruited the wrong guy..." Her mind whirled with the endless chances of disaster. "If one cop got killed, Joe, all because I didn't want to have a fight with my husband about traveling..." She shook her head; she couldn't let that happen.

Joe considered what she had said for a moment. "Okay." He glanced over at her. "But what if it does come down to a choice? What if it comes down to Rick or FORS, or setting up some new program and Rick—what're you gonna do?"

Midnight gave him a sharp look, then her face clouded with concern. Joe knew Rick better than anyone, maybe even better than her. "Do you think it would come to that? Is he really that possessive?"

Joe shrugged. "He can be. It's never really been over a woman before, because before you, all his relationships were kept very casual. But now..." He shrugged again. "You're different, you mean everything to him, and maybe he can't see past that. I don't know what he'll do."

"Do you think he'd let it come to divorce?"

"Maybe."

"But if he loves me so much, and if I'm so important to him..."

Joe shook his head. "Night, Rick is a 'my way or no way' kind of guy." He saw Midnight grinning, nodding. "And," he added, "if you think I was bad, you ain't seen nothin'. You don't realize how far Rick will go to get his way if he really wants something. But I don't honestly think he believes that it would go that far. His ego's probably telling him that if you think you'll lose him then you'll back off on the trips."

Again Midnight nodded. "I think you're right."

"Of course I am," Joe said smugly. "Trick here is, that like I've tried to tell him before, he hasn't dealt with any woman like you before. He's never had a woman get the better of him, or even really try."

"I thought he knew who I was when he married me, Joe," Midnight said angrily.

"And I'll wager that you thought you knew him, didn't you?"

"Got me there," Midnight said. Joe nodded, smirking. "Okay, so enough about my problems. What happened with you and Randy? Are you still being an asshole?"

Joe laughed. Only Midnight would go straight to the heart of such a touchy subject for him. "Thanks, Night, I love you too," he said, still smiling. He nodded slowly. "Yeah, I guess I am a little bit, but mostly it's Randy." Midnight glanced at him cynically. "Well, it is! She's not talking to me."

"Serves you right," Midnight said. Joe had told her what he had said to Randy, and Midnight had told him that if he'd said that to her she would have knocked his block off.

"Yeah, yeah, I know," Joe said, his expression indicating that he had heard it before. "I'm a male chauvinist pig, and I don't deserve to live, and if you were married to me you'd have shot me a long time ago," he recited as if by rote, rolling his eyes. They were parked in front of Midnight and Rick's house now, and Joe had turned off the engine.

55

"Damn straight," Midnight said, grinning. "But I love you anyway. So are you going to try to make up, or are you just going to wait her out?"

Joe looked recalcitrant. "I guess I could try and make up, but I'm not gonna kiss up. She was wrong a little bit."

"Yeah, God forbid she didn't ask your permission first."

"Alright already, I get it," he said, nodding like a schoolboy.

"Good." Midnight leaned over and gave him a quick kiss on the cheek. "And thank you for coming to my rescue." She went to open the car door—his hand on her arm stopped her.

"You gonna be okay?" he asked, concern on his face.

"Oh yeah," Midnight said, waving away his worries with her hand. "I'm goin' to bed, and as far as I'm concerned, the asshole can sleep on the couch."

Joe laughed, knowing Midnight was just ornery enough to follow through. "May be where I end up one of these days—on your couch, that is."

Midnight laughed as she got out of the car, leaning down to look at him. "Anytime, honey. Anytime." She closed the door and waved as she walked up to the house. Joe watched until she was safely inside then waited an extra few minutes, until he saw her wave from the living room window. The incident over three years ago, when Rick had left her at her house without waiting the extra time and she had been attacked, had made both Joe and Rick paranoid about dropping her off. Midnight had argued with them about it for a while, but had long since given up. Joe drove home, thinking all the while about what he was going to do about Randy.

****

When Joe returned home, he noted that Randy had gone to bed while he'd been gone; she'd been in the living room when he came out of their bedroom. He knew she was mad at him, but he didn't know exactly what to do about it. He didn't want her to think he condoned the idea of her becoming a police officer, because he didn't, and he knew he really couldn't. He also didn't want her to stay mad at him. Joe realized how much Randy had become such an integral part of his life. Before Randy he'd had work, and sometimes he and Midnight had been a thing, but basically it was always connected to work. Randy was something separate, something different from what he dealt with at work, and he realized the selfish part of him wanted to keep it that way. He also knew that wasn't fair to Randy—she had a right to a career too. But why this one? But he thought he already knew that. It was Joe's feeling that Randy had idolized Midnight from the first time they had met, and now Randy was trying, in some small way, to become more like Midnight. He wasn't cocky enough to believe it was to be more attractive to him; he knew that wasn't the case. Randy had seemed to want more lately. She seemed to be pulling away from him, and the cocoon he had tried to wrap her in; she seemed to want to be independent of him, so much so that she would go so far as to apply to be a police officer behind his back, knowing he wouldn't like it.

The problem was, what should he do? He didn't want her to be a police officer. In truth, if he really chose to look at it, he didn't want her to be independent of him either, but he knew that wasn't right or fair to her.

Walking into their bedroom, Joe took note of the fact that her back was to him, and that she was tense—she wasn't asleep. He put his keys on his dresser, took off the jacket he had thrown on over his sweats and T-shirt to go and pick up Midnight, also removing the small handgun he had shoved into the deep pockets of the jacket. Kicking off his shoes, he climbed into bed and lay on his back for a few minutes. He could feel Randy tense further as he rolled onto his side, facing her back. He reached out, touching her waist, nuzzling the back of her head with his lips.

"I'm a shit," he muttered into her hair, "so shoot me."

He almost felt her grin, and she relaxed against him. He hugged her closer to him. She turned over to face him, her eyes searching his face in the dim light. "You still don't want me to do it, do you?"

Joe hesitated, but he knew he couldn't lie to her. Slowly, he shook his head. "No, but I won't try to stop you either. It's your decision, and I guess I'll just have to deal with it as it comes."

Randy smiled. "I guess that's about the best I'm going to get, huh?"

"Just about."

"Well, I love you anyway."

"Gee, thanks." He grinned.

Joe leaned down and kissed her, and all their arguments melted away. They both slept much better that evening, their argument resolved for the time being.

****

Midnight was not so lucky, however. Rick stumbled into their bedroom around two o'clock in the morning. It was very obvious that he was drunk, but he tried to hide it. Midnight was lying in bed on her side, facing him. She opened one eye when he came into the room, the light from the hallway pouring in around him.

"Had a good time, did we?" Midnight said.

Rick gave her a sour look. "Well, one of us had to."

Midnight sighed dramatically. "Oh, the sacrifices you do make."

"More than you can claim," Rick replied snidely.

"Ah yes, I know." Midnight sat up, her copper-gold hair falling all around her shoulders. She set her expression to that of an apologetic schoolgirl. "I was a bad, bad girl, and just for that I won't get to go to any more fancy parties." Her voice was that of a little girl's, but the sarcasm it dripped was all woman. Then she narrowed her eyes at Rick. "I could be so fucking lucky."

Rick stared at her openmouthed. Apparently he hadn't expected this tactic from her; he had obviously thought she would be sincerely apologetic.

"So, I take it you're proud of your behavior this evening?" he asked, his voice reflecting his surprise.

Midnight pursed her lips as if she were considering the question, then muttered, "Well, I guess I could have just stood up and shot the bastard, but that would have been a little much, don't you think?"

"I don't believe you!" Rick hollered. "You actually think you had some sort of right to act the way you did?"

"And I guess I could say that I don't believe you," Midnight said sharply. "You actually expected me to react any other way?"

"You know, Midnight, the whole world doesn't have to think the way you do."

"No, they don't, but they have to at least be armed when it comes to having a battle of wits," she snapped.

"For your information," Rick said, sounding every bit the aristocrat, "Mr. Theland is a very well-educated man."

Midnight shrugged. "Yeah, but not when it comes to the real world. Life is not lived inside the hallowed halls of Oxford, you know."

"Yes, I know, but could we at least get out of the ghetto every now and then?"

"Feel free, just don't take me with you."

Rick raised an eyebrow. "Well, I don't think you'll have to worry about the local society matrons beating down your door."

"Oh, and that really breaks my heart," Midnight said, a look of mock distress on her face.

"I'm sure." Rick turned to leave the room, slamming the door on the way out. Midnight sat looking at the door for a long few minutes, her eyes burning with anger. She couldn't believe that not only had he not stood up for her, but he actually sided with them.

After a few minutes she lay back down, and after about an hour of tossing and turning, she fell into a fitful sleep.

The next morning she woke feeling more tired than she had when she'd gone to bed. It was not going to be a good day, she could just tell.

Upon coming into the kitchen she found that Rick had slept on the couch, and had apparently told his sister he had something to do and had showered and left early. Mikeyla, sensing that something was wrong, clung to Midnight and wouldn't let herself be put down.

Deborah knew Rick was enraged about Midnight's behavior the night before, and she also knew Rick had spent the rest of the evening drinking and having long, quiet conversations with Sheila. Deborah was quite perturbed with her brother for having acted the way he had, and for not going after his wife when she left. Deborah had gone over to Rick when he reentered the dining room, and asked where Midnight had gone.

Rick had shrugged "She left," he said, sounding very unconcerned.

"How did she leave, Richard?" Deborah asked. "You have the car keys, don't you?"

Rick gave his sister a sour look, then said, "You have no idea how resourceful my wife can be." It was as if he were loath to give Midnight any credit.

"I see," Deborah said. "And that's your excuse for not going after her?"

"Quite," Rick snapped, then walked away.

Deborah had been surprised at her brother's tone; she had literally been stunned into a shocked silence. She watched him the rest of the evening, but did not say another word to him. Wilson had sensed her shocked dismay and attempted to be more attentive to her than usual, hoping to reset the balance. He hated to have anything out of balance; it was the banker in him.

Now, as Deborah looked at Midnight as she held Mikeyla, not even touching her coffee, she could tell she was tired and upset, and she surmised that Midnight and Rick had had some words when he dragged himself home early that morning. He had given the keys to his car to Deborah around eleven o'clock the night before and told her he'd catch a ride home with someone. Deborah was pretty sure she could guess who that someone would be. It bothered her greatly that her brother was being so reckless with his marriage, but she knew she would have no real influence on him; Katherine had been the only one who ever had, and Katherine would never push Midnight over someone like Sheila Theland. Sheila was what Katherine would consider good Debenshire stock. So Deborah knew that she had to try, even if she didn't help anything.

Later that day, Midnight had gone off to take a nap. Rick had not returned by 1:00 p.m., but had called and said he would be home by 2:00. Deborah noted that Midnight seemed to time her nap for right about fifteen minutes before Rick was to be home. But she decided this would be a good time to talk to her brother. So, leaving her daughters happily engaged in play with Mikeyla and Wilson working happily on his laptop, Deborah all but dragged her brother out to the deck overlooking the ocean.

Rick sat on one of the lounge chairs, looking out at the sea. His dark blue eyes were very wary; he was sure he knew what was coming. His light brown curls, long and shaggy, blew in the light breeze from the ocean. Deborah couldn't help but be aware of how good-looking her brother really was. His handsome features were only the beginning of his assets; Deborah knew her brother had a charming personality, a quick wit, and a great depth of emotion that he allowed the people closest to him see often. It was his nature to feel everything very deeply, to take everything to heart and express in one form or another his feelings about any given issue.

His expressions didn't always take a verbal form; more often than not they were physical. Deborah remembered the time he had been forced to go to a debutante ball. He had shown up an hour late, half-crocked, his tuxedo shirt half unbuttoned, with black jeans and a leather jacket and boots. He had proceeded to flirt outrageously with all of the debutantes, causing many of them to either blush furiously or all but eat out of his hand. He basically accosted the girl he was supposed to escort and took her riding, in her ball gown, on his motorcycle. Then he had brought her back two days later, and no one was sure to that day what they had done or where they had gone, but the girl had never had an unkind word to say about him; nor would she reveal their secret. That girl had been Sheila Theland. That was what worried Deborah the most. Rick had a past with this girl, and she was afraid he was trying to recapture something he remembered fondly from his youthful days of being free and wild.

Deborah watched her brother for a few minutes, silent to the point of making him sigh loudly.

"What is it, Deb?" he asked.

"I think you know, Richard."

Rick nodded at her slowly. He looked tired.

"What is it you think you're doing with Sheila Theland?" she asked, raising a disapproving eyebrow.

Rick looked at her for a long, measured moment, then shrugged casually. "I'm just havin' a good time."

"I see." Deborah sounded very much like their mother at that moment. "And?"

"And what?" Rick said, a rush of frustration pushing him to his feet. He walked over to the rail and looked out at the ocean. "I'm just havin' fun, Deb, that's all."

"What kind of fun, Richard?"

Rick didn't answer right away, and he wouldn't look at his sister. "Nothin', Deb," he said eventually. "Really."

Deborah looked at him again, trying to decide if he was not telling her the truth to keep her from having to lie to Midnight, or if he was really being honest.

"Do I hear 'not yet' in that statement?" she asked finally.

Rick looked at her. "You think it's easy?" He gestured toward the house and his wife within. "To live with that? To live with someone who cares more about her damn job than she does anything else? To watch her every day, trying to clean up the garbage that just keeps coming? To see her have to kiss up to guys who would just love to get her in bed, and to watch her have to tap-dance just out of their reach and call it politics?" He turned back to the railing, his eyes swimming with unshed tears of anger. "I hate it," he said. "I hate it, and sometimes..."

Deborah waited, but when he didn't continue, she said softly, soothingly, "Sometimes what, Richard?" She'd never seen her brother this emotional over any woman.

"Sometimes," he began, pausing as he closed his eyes and swallowed. Then he opened his eyes and looked at his sister. When he spoke again, his voice was so quiet she could barely hear it over the sound of the crashing waves. "Sometimes I hate her."

Deborah was shocked, and all she could think to do was hug her brother. She knew she had no words to say that could help him, and

64

she didn't know what she could do. She knew Rick was hurting, and she knew his hurt was hurting Midnight, but she couldn't fix it. The thought made her feel helpless, and she prayed that somewhere, somehow, Rick and Midnight could get through this. Deborah also knew that for Rick to feel the way he did about Midnight's job, he must love his wife very deeply. She just hoped his actions in reaction to Midnight's work wouldn't be more than their marriage could take.

CHAPTER 4

The rest of Deborah's stay flew by, and it seemed like no time at all before Midnight, Rick, and Mikeyla were taking them to the airport to say goodbye. Mikeyla held Susan's hand as they headed toward the gate. Wilson was carrying Liz, walking behind the meandering pair. Rick and Deborah were walking side by side. Midnight was behind them all, with her hands in the pocket of her FORS jacket. Deborah had tried to talk to Midnight about what Rick had said, and about what she thought her brother was feeling, but Midnight hadn't really understood. She had said that Rick shouldn't have a problem with her job, and that she'd had the job before she had him. Deborah had gently suggested that perhaps Midnight should cut back on some of her hours, maybe be home more.

Midnight had been infuriated, getting very defensive about how much time she spent at home, saying she didn't appreciate being treated as the bad guy. "I wasn't the one who stayed out till two in the morning getting wasted, and with an ex-girlfriend to boot!" she had all but yelled.

The conversation had basically ended there. Midnight would not listen, and a small, independent part of Deborah didn't blame her.

Deborah couldn't even begin to grasp how hard this change in lifestyle was for Midnight. Midnight had always been her own person, and had always had all the freedom she wanted, extracting what she wanted from life with no major responsibilities except, of course, for

FORS. Having to worry about another person's feelings and problems as well as taking care of her daughter's needs was really a lot to deal with, and now Rick was going to start being difficult about FORS? Midnight knew she was going to have to draw the line somewhere if she wanted to retain any of herself, and if Rick got his feelings hurt, tough.

The goodbyes were hardest on Mikeyla. She had become very fond of Susan during their stay, and she didn't understand why she had to leave. By the time they boarded the plane, Mikeyla was in tears and Midnight had to hold her to keep her from running down the gangway after Susan and the family. Deborah had hugged her brother and then Midnight, telling her she hoped everything worked out. Midnight had nodded numbly. She felt bad that she had been so angry with Deborah when they had talked about Rick, but she couldn't bring herself to apologize either. So Deborah, Wilson, Susan, and Liz boarded the plane on their way back home, and Midnight, Rick, and Mikeyla walked back to the car in silence.

Within minutes of getting into the car, Mikeyla was asleep. The silence seemed to expand. When Midnight couldn't take it anymore she reached over and turned on the radio. Journey's "Message of Love" was playing, and Midnight wanted to laugh as she listened to the chorus. Listening to Steve Perry ask if his baby could hear him, if she could hear his message of love.

Midnight thought those words really seemed to fit their situation pretty well. She knew they were in trouble, but she didn't know how to fix it. If Rick was upset about her commitment to FORS then there really was a problem. The trouble was that Midnight was not willing to give up FORS—not for Rick, not for anyone… except maybe for Mikeyla, she thought, glancing back at her sleeping daughter.

A few minutes later Rick's cell phone rang. He answered it on the hands-free.

"Richard?" a woman with a distinctly familiar English accent queried.

"Yes?" Rick said, smiling. Midnight's eyes narrowed.

"Richard, I'm glad I got you," she exclaimed happily, having no idea that his wife was listening.

"What's goin' on?" he asked, glancing at Midnight to see how she was taking the fact that his ex-girlfriend was calling him.

She stared back at him, her face devoid of emotion, but the look in her eyes was one of cold anger. Rick reached over and picked up the phone, canceling hands-free, not sure what Sheila wanted but aware that it was probably something Midnight didn't need to hear.

Rick was very obviously trying to keep the conversation one-sided, so Midnight didn't know what Sheila was saying. She felt herself growing colder, and angrier; she wanted to reach over and snatch the phone out of Rick's hand, and tell the little limey bitch to get her own man. But Midnight was nothing if not very controlled; she had gotten very good at hiding her impulsiveness and keeping her cool. Dealing with the heads of large police departments and sheriffs' units had taught her that.

Dragging her attention forcefully away from Rick's conversation, Midnight thought about her upcoming trip to Sacramento. She was scheduled to talk to some of the heads of the state-level Bureau of Investigations and some at the Bureau of Narcotic Enforcement's Violence Suppression team as well. She was excited about the prospect of talking to other law enforcement officials about policies and strategies. She was very proud of the unit she had built, and still constantly surprised at other agencies' reactions to both her program and to her in general. Midnight's petite stature and surprising good looks tended to set what Midnight liked to call the cop-types back a few paces. In a way she now enjoyed surprising them; before FORS had become so successful, her appearance had been more of a hindrance than a help, but now, bringing up FORS' success statistics was a good way to smooth over officials' ruffled feathers.

Midnight had begun to feel this trip to Sacramento might help ease things a bit with Rick, and maybe make him miss her a little bit. She was slated to leave two days hence; she had already made arrangements to have Mikeyla taken care of by an au pair. Deborah had contacted the agency and had them send information on the au pairs they had under their employment. Midnight had read the information and tried to get Rick's input on who they should hire, but he had been uninterested, telling Midnight that she should be able to make that decision on her own. He snidely recited a recent description of her in the local newspaper referring to her as "the head of a highly successful law enforcement team." Midnight made the choice with cold resignation, knowing that Rick was just being a jerk. She would be happy to remind him of the conversation should he bring up any flaws in her decision-making abilities.

Rick finally hung up the cell phone after about five minutes of stilted conversation. He returned his attention to his driving, as if the call had never happened. The rest of the drive was quiet; neither was willing to give in and say something to break the silence. When they got home, Midnight got Mikeyla out of her car seat and took her into the house. She laid her down on her bed and shut her door.

She walked into her and Rick's bedroom, where he was changing clothes. She wanted to ask him where he was going, but she didn't. She knew he was waiting for her to ask, and she didn't want to be predictable. Shrugging inwardly, Midnight picked up a report she'd been wanting to read and walked out of the room.

Rick found her a half hour later, sitting on the couch in their den. She had her feet tucked under her, a highlighter pen between her teeth, engrossed in her report. The stereo was on, playing the soundtrack from *Twister* on compact disc. It was on Van Halen's "Humans Being"; the words "You wonder why your life is screaming, wonder why we're humans being" made Rick grin sardonically. That was exactly how he felt at this moment. Sheila had texted him to invite him to a party at a club in La Jolla. She had told him a few people he knew would be there, and that he'd have a good time. She had also told him he could bring his wife; she had said the word as if it were distasteful to her. The idea to bring Midnight itself seemed an afterthought. In reality, Sheila had suddenly realized that inviting Rick wouldn't be considered appropriate if she didn't invite his wife too; she didn't want to appear unseemly, even if she really only wanted Rick to be there.

****

Sheila Theland knew all the ins and outs of high society. She knew how to use insinuation and coquettish wiles to get anything she wanted, and right now she wanted one Richard Debenshire. To Sheila's way of thinking, someone as uncouth as Rick's wife didn't have a right to be married to a member of upper English society. The Debenshire family had been considered higher society simply because Robert Debenshire represented many important clients such as Joseph Sinclair's family. A lot of people had been shocked and appalled when Joe saw fit to marry so low-income a nobody from America—and she had been a child, no less! Sheila still found that appalling, as well as his choice of what Sheila considered a distraction—that job he had! Sheila's father was of the same mind, hence the lack of invitations to the Sinclair household. Not that the reprehensible couple seemed affected by the Thelands' disassociation, but Sheila was sure Joseph Michael Sinclair would rue the day he married the little tart. It didn't bother her that she had never met Randy Sinclair; she felt she knew all she needed to know, which she had garnered from her father's statements.

Sheila had grown up in a household that did things the old society way. She had been taught to be ladylike and graceful. She didn't have to worry about her future, because whatever happened, she knew her father would always take care of her. As a teen, Sheila Theland had set her sights on Richard Debenshire. Her father had been less than pleased, because Richard Debenshire was a hoodlum, and therefore beneath Sheila's considerations. But Sheila had heard about Rick's wild side, and she liked the idea of taming him; his sharp good looks and long hair excited her own wild side. It never occurred to her that he had a reputation as a player for a reason, and had she stopped to think about it, she would have shrugged and said that was with "other women," not her.

Sheila had pursued Rick as she had never pursued a man before. When he finally took her up on her many suggestions she had been totally flustered; it was not something she was used to. Rick had kept her guessing during their tumultuous six-month relationship. She had come to think of him as fire; the closer she got, the harder she tried to contain him, the more she got burned and the more pain she felt. In the end she had told him she thought she was pregnant, in a last desperate attempt to hold on to him. She hadn't been sure that she was; in fact, she had only been two days late.

His reaction to her revelation wasn't what she had been prepared for. She had expected either out and out anger or sullen resignation— she received neither. He had stared at her for a moment, then off into space for a long time. She could see he was considering his options. Then he nodded imperceptibly, as if he had just made an agreement with himself. To her utter shock he stood up and left, and she didn't hear from him again for two weeks. When he eventually showed up at her parents' door he was dressed in his customary jeans, black cotton button-up shirt, and leather jacket. He asked for her and stood leaning indolently against the doorjamb, preventing the butler from closing the door.

The butler had told Sheila Mr. Debenshire was there to call on her, and she had frantically tried to straighten herself up; she had been crying only moments before, thinking she had lost him forever. She had run around her room, trying to look like she hadn't been doing just that. As she rushed down the elegantly appointed hallway of her parents' home, she told herself she would be cool and unaffected by him, punishing him for his rebuff.

Reaching the top of the stairs, almost breathless, she looked down at him and saw him waiting patiently, calmly, almost bored. All she had wanted to do was make him smile at her again. As she rushed down the stairs, all her dignity and cavalier attitudes went by the wayside, and she became the person she abhorred most—a desperate, submissive, love-struck teenager. When she got to him, she threw her arms around him and kissed him on the cheek, sensing that if she tried to kiss him on the lips he wouldn't return it. She took his hand and led him into the sitting room. He sat on the sofa, leaning back against the expensive damask cushions, regarding her calmly.

"So?" he had said simply, one eyebrow raised cynically.

"So?" Sheila replied, almost stupidly, then realized what he was asking. "Oh!" She was startled that he would be so crass as to bring up a subject of such a delicate nature so casually, as if he were asking after something as everyday as the weather.

When she didn't respond to his question, he narrowed his eyes, his mouth pursing in anger held in check. *At least*, she had thought, *he isn't rude enough to actually ask the question outright.* She was always making excuses for his attitude and demeanor. She also knew she shouldn't continue to play games with him, that she should tell him what he wanted to know, but she just couldn't believe that was the only reason he had come. Surely he had missed her too.

"I've missed you a great deal," she said, smiling shyly at him, pretending not to understand what he was asking. Hoping his refined behavior wouldn't allow him to ask her directly, and that she could get him interested in her again in the meantime.

Rick didn't respond. He just watched her, his deep blue eyes cool, his expression showing that he was unaffected by her. Finally, she shook her head, her eyes on the floor. Somehow she had expected him to breathe a sigh of relief and tell her to be more careful, that they could get back to their relationship. But once again, he surprised her, standing up and walking out without one word. She didn't hear from him for over two months, until they ran into each other at a party his parents had forced him to attend. He and Joe were there together, and they were loud, rude; their behavior was beyond reprehensible. When she caught him alone at one point, he looked at her as if he didn't even know her. She had been devastated, but had managed to convince herself since then that he had only been drunk, and that was why he pretended not to recognize her.

Sheila had no idea what she had put him through, mentioning a possible pregnancy with such a casual air. She had sent him into a tailspin; he had seen his life spiraling out of control over someone he didn't even love. He could see having to marry her, and being stuck in a miserable marriage, all because he had sex with the wrong person at the wrong time.

****

Somehow all of the past seemed to have slipped away, and much like with any experience, especially from the carefree days of youth, over time he seemed only to remember how much fun he'd had. Something in the back of his mind was nagging him as he picked up his keys and headed out the door, making a point of not looking back to see if Midnight was watching. If he had looked, he would have seen that she was watching, her face drawn and unhappy. Then again, if he'd looked, she may have changed her expression so as to appear unaffected by what he was so obviously doing.

After Rick left, Midnight sat and listened to music. She remembered all the fun times she and Rick had had, and how they seemed so well matched. *We are well matched*, she thought wryly. *Too well matched. We're almost exactly the same.* She shook her head, wondering what was going to happen to them, unsure how to stop this out-of-control ride they were on. Knowing the ride had to end somewhere, but afraid to even think of where.

74

Midnight fell asleep on the couch and slept fitfully until 3:00 a.m., when she woke to the sound of the front door closing. She sat up, unaware of how young she looked, all tousled from sleep, the sleeves of her oversized shirt coming down over her hands as she rubbed her eyes. Rick stood looking at her from the entryway, suddenly feeling horribly guilty about having such a good time, feeling like what he had just done was going to end everything between him and Midnight. And desperately afraid that it would. But as Midnight glanced at the clock on the VCR and then at him, her face set in a cynical "I told you so" mask, Rick felt the anger well up in him. He knew he didn't have a right to be mad at her; he knew what he was feeling was anger at himself, for tearing apart the only thing that really meant anything to him, but he was unable to keep his mouth shut.

"You have a problem?" he asked, his voice dripping with sarcasm.

Midnight looked at him for a long moment, shook her head almost sadly, and then stood up. Walking right by him, she headed down the hallway to their bedroom and closed the door very quietly.

Rick stared after her, surprised at her reaction, unsure of what to do next. In his ambivalent state, he headed over to their liquor cabinet. There wasn't much in it; Midnight and he weren't really the hard liquor types. But he found a bottle of vodka used to make watermelon shooters, and he took a long, burning swig. *Aren't I reverting to my old habits, and doesn't that just make me so mature?* he thought derisively. He shook his head, knowing he was being ridiculous, but not willing to *feel* ridiculous and go in and grovel to Midnight. *Part of this is her fault*, he told himself, feeling ever so slightly vindicated. *Serves her right.* He took another long swig from the bottle he held cradled against his chest. *Great*, a more rational part of his mind answered. *And this will show her.*

"Shut up," Rick said out loud. Then he chuckled. *Great, now I'm starting to sound like one of the drunks in Hyde Park.* Shutting down his senses, he proceeded to get drunk and pass out on the couch.

Meanwhile, Midnight leaned against the bedroom door—she had made a grand effort not to slam it—staring blindly at the far wall. She felt torn up inside, not wanting to know where Rick had gone, or with whom. But she was aware all the while that she did know, that she just wouldn't let herself think about it right now. Like Scarlett O'Hara said in that all-time great motion picture, "I'll think about it tomorrow."

"Yeah," Midnight said, moving to lie down on the bed, "and look what that got her. Rhett left in the end anyway."

She thought about it for a while, and realized it only made her want to go out and pound on Rick's head or scream at him for hours on end. She decided that would not solve anything. *Whaddya know,* she thought, laughing to herself. *The kid may grow up yet.* She knew that was what Tom would say. Tom was her oldest and dearest friend, and at times he seemed to be the only person she could count on for a pick-me-up. Even Joe had his own problems now. Midnight wondered vaguely what was happening with Randy's application for the PD; she made a mental note to check on it the next day.

CHAPTER 5

Randy had continued through the hiring process with San Diego Police Department. She had talked about it very little with Joe; she knew it was a very sore subject and best left alone. Just when things had gotten back to normal, with less tension between them, Randy got the word that a background check was being done on her. That usually meant a shoo-in for the candidate, unless there was something questionable in their background. With Randy, there was less than nothing questionable. Her husband was a sergeant with the department, and her two closest friends, Midnight and Rick, were also police officers, so things were pretty sure.

Randy got the call from her background investigator and immediately went to Joe's office—she wanted him to hear it from her. When she walked in it was obvious that he had already heard. His face could have been carved out of stone, his chin resting on his fist, his elbow on his desk. He stared right at her from the minute she walked in the door, his expression unemotional, almost passive, but Randy knew better. She'd been with Joe for over three years now, and she knew that with him, calm usually meant anything but passivity.

"You heard?" she asked quietly, hating herself just a little bit for being so meek. He nodded slowly, his jaw set in controlled anger, as she sat in the chair across from his desk.

How many times had she sat in this exact place, happily talking to her husband, feeling so special because he had chosen her above all the women he had dated before? They had talked about everything in this office. Even about having children, once; Midnight had had Mikeyla at work that day, and Randy had felt a particular pull of desire to have a little baby of her own. She'd walked into Joe's office all dreamy-eyed, and Joe had started laughing the moment he saw her.

"What?" she had asked him, smiling shyly.

"What?" he repeated, still smiling broadly. "I know what's made you all doe-eyed—you're lookin' at Night's kid and you want one too." His eyes had sparkled when he said it, and Randy knew then that he wanted it too. They had spent half the afternoon talking about it, whether this was the right time, how they would handle the daycare issue. Randy had come away from the conversation feeling very loved and very happy.

But now, things were not so happy. If she became a police officer, she certainly couldn't have children right now. It struck her that her decision for a career had had yet another impact on her life. It hadn't really occurred to her at the time that applying for and becoming a police officer meant she wasn't going to have children any time soon. The thought nagged at her while she sat waiting to hear what Joe would say about the whole thing. A tiny bit of her, a part she wouldn't even begin to recognize, was hoping Joe would say she couldn't do it so things could go back to normal with them, but the rest of her was ready to battle him if he tried to stop her.

She waited in silence for what seemed like forever. She knew saying something to him right now would probably ignite his anger. Joe was like a smoldering ember when he was mad, and he just needed someone to blow on that ember to make it flare up into rage. Randy had long since learned not to be the person to wake the fire. So she continued to wait. But before Joe said anything, Midnight came in; she wasn't just a slight breeze on Joe's anger—she was basically a gust of wind.

"Hey!" Midnight said gleefully, walking over to Randy and shaking her. "I heard you made it!"

Randy didn't say anything. She just looked up at Midnight and smiled weakly. Joe all but flew out of his chair.

"How the fuck do you know already?" he growled, his eyes narrowed at Randy as if she had told Midnight before coming to tell him.

Midnight gazed back at her partner of many years, not batting an eyelash at Joe's anger, nor his grossly insubordinate behavior. She had dealt with Joe in this kind of state many times before.

She shrugged casually. "Probably the same way you did." Her voice was so calm and even that Joe didn't say another word. He just sank back into his chair, blowing his breath out in a rush. He shook his head again, as if Midnight knowing Randy was "in" made it true beyond any doubt. He looked at Randy, his eyes daring her to defy him. He said a single word, his voice low, certainly not indicating that he expected a negative reply. "So?"

Randy looked from Joe to Midnight, then back to Joe. She had seen encouragement in the other woman's eyes, and drew in a deep breath. "I'm taking it." Her voice held the slightest tremor, but her expression showed determination.

Joe was silent again. He looked at Midnight, noting that she was ready and willing to do battle on Randy's behalf. He nodded, but Randy could see he just didn't plan on taking on both Randy and Midnight—he'd wait. She almost dreaded the ride home that evening. She didn't like to fight with anyone, least of all Joe. In the few fights they'd had, Randy had seen that Joe could be ruthless if he really believed in what he was fighting for—or against. She knew, too, that Joe was very much against her becoming a police officer, and she knew why, but she didn't feel that she should be stymied because of the death of Joe's parents so many years ago.

So she waited. The rest of the day seemed to fly by, punctuated by a few small incidents that mostly stemmed from Joe's anger at her. He flew off the handle at one of the newer members of FORS because the young man had taken a dangerous chance in the field, an action that could have easily resulted in his injury or death, which served to further polarize Joe's concern about losing people he cared about. Midnight became part of the altercation, simply due to her position as the boss. Even knowing what she did about Joe's current state of mind, she tried to reason with him, saying he would have done the same thing. Joe had left her office, slamming the door.

The rest of the day didn't go much better. Before Randy knew it, it was time to go home. Joe walked out of his office with his jacket on and keys in hand. He went to speak to Midnight for a few minutes, then walked toward the elevators. Randy stood up and followed him. This was not going to be a fun ride home—she knew that already, just from the set of his jaw and the stiff way he moved. Joe didn't wear seething well; one could always tell how he was feeling.

The walk to the car was silent. Joe didn't take her hand as he usually did, but Randy didn't really expect him to. Joe pushed a CD into the player and Def Leppard's album *Slang* started out of the speakers. "All I Want Is Everything" was playing a few minutes later as Joe got on the freeway toward La Jolla. As he always did when a song fit his feelings, Joe reached over and turned it up. The words seemed to have been written for their lives at this moment. It talked about how hard things could get in a relationship when one party wanted so much and the other wasn't willing to give it, asking if wanting everything was asking too much. Joe wanted to know if he was asking too much to want his wife safe.

Randy knew Joe was really feeling the song's words, and she felt the same. They needed to talk, but she was afraid that discussing it would make them come to a decision, that it might make him say "the job or me," and Randy didn't know what to do. She wanted to talk, but she also didn't want to hear what he would say.

Joe turned the radio down after the song ended, but he still didn't say anything. Finally Randy couldn't take it anymore, even though she knew he was waiting her out and she was giving in to him.

"So, are you never going to speak to me again?"

Joe glanced at her, his expression very serious. He didn't feel like he'd have won anything if she knew, if he could tell her he was feeling exactly as she was. He was hoping that by not talking about it, it would just go away. He wanted to wish it away.

"What do you want me to say?" he asked quietly.

"Something, anything," she said, angry at him for putting her in this position.

"Tell me what you think I should say."

"I don't know, Joe. It's not like you didn't know I was applying. You knew I was doing this."

Joe's mouth twisted in a sardonic grin. "Oh yeah, I knew."

"And did you think I wouldn't get the job, or were you just hoping I wouldn't?" she said, her anger rising. Joe thought fleetingly that she sounded a lot like Midnight.

"Hoping, I guess," he answered honestly.

"I see." Randy shook her head. "So you're the only one that's allowed to have a career, is that it?"

"Oh God!" Joe exclaimed, his accent thick. "Is that what you think? You think I just don't want you to be a cop because I think so much of my *career*? You have got to be kidding. I'm worried about *you*, not my ego."

Randy felt the need to say something hateful in the wake of his admission. "Well, I guess it's hard to tell these days."

"Hard to tell what? That I care? What's that supposed to mean? You think I don't care about you anymore?" Joe looked perplexed; he hadn't thought of it that way before.

"Well, you certainly haven't been supportive lately," Randy said, sounding hurt.

Joe shook his head, then glanced at her again. "What do you want me to do? You want me to say that your becoming a cop is a great idea? Well I can't, and I won't."

"So what does this mean?" Randy's eyes were filling with tears, partially from anger and partially from all the other emotions she'd been feeling since she got the word that she was basically hired.

"I don't know what it means," Joe said, sounding tired.

Randy was silent for a moment, not sure if she wanted to say the words that were on her tongue, before speaking hesitantly. "Okay, so if I take the job, does that mean, well, are we over?"

Joe looked at her sharply, surprised that she even had the nerve to bring it up. It had been spinning around in his mind, ricocheting off of his memories of his parents and the anguish their death had caused, but also off his feelings for Randy, which were so deep.

Finally, he shook his head sadly. "I don't know."

"Well, where does that leave me then?"

"What do you want? Do you want me to predict the future?"

"No, I want to know where we stand," she said, again sounding a lot like Midnight.

"Look," Joe said as he exited the freeway. "I don't know how I'm gonna feel about it—I can't tell you. All I can say is that I don't want you to be a cop."

"Well, I want to take the job."

"And that's your decision." Joe shrugged.

"But then we're over." Randy sounded angrier and a lot less unhappy this time.

"And that's what I can't tell you. I don't know what will happen."

"But you're going to hold this over my head, right?"

"Jesus Christ, Randy, what do you want for my life?" He was yelling, his voice strident. "I told you, this is how I feel about the whole thing, and where you go from there is your decision. I'm not going to say I think it's a good idea, because I don't, but I won't stop you either. But I'm not going to guarantee you that this won't screw things up with us."

Randy was quiet. She was looking for reassurance, but Joe was not providing it. She felt very alone at that moment, and she didn't know what to do to change that.

A few minutes later Joe pulled up to their house. He got out of the car, and out of sheer habit walked around to get her door for her, but she had already opened it. Joe took a step back, putting his hands up, palms out, to indicate futility. He turned and walked toward the house, his long legs carrying him there long before Randy got there; she was purposely meandering. At the front door, he punched in the security code and heard the locks click open. He walked in, allowing the door to close behind him, which was also out of character; he had been brought up in a very proper English household, and that upbringing made it all but compulsory for him to act the gentleman whenever possible. Randy knew it took a real effort for him to ignore his discipline.

Joe walked straight to the bar and poured a shot of whiskey, drank it, then poured another. Turning around, he saw Randy watching him from the door. He shook his head and headed for their bedroom.

Half an hour later, Randy was in the kitchen, trying to decide whether she should cook for them. She hadn't planned anything since it was Friday, when they usually went out to dinner or ordered in. Joe walked into the kitchen, having checked a few other rooms first; he was carrying his gun. He had changed his shirt and was wearing his bulletproof vest over it. He had switched to a belt holster for his gun. Randy looked up at him.

"So I guess that answers my question about dinner," she said blandly.

Joe grinned. "Yeah, I guess."

"What do you have?" Randy was happy to be having a civilized conversation with him, after the argument they'd had earlier.

"Search warrant," Joe replied, pulling back the slide on his gun to chamber a round then holstering it. "I shouldn't be too late." He looked down at her and saw the sadness in her eyes; it was reflected in his. He stepped forward, gathering her into his arms. She rested her head against his chest and sighed.

"Are we going to make it through this?" she said, knowing she was repeating the same question she'd asked in the car, and wondering belatedly if he'd get mad again. But Joe seemed to take the question differently this time, the way she'd meant it—she wasn't asking for guarantees, just some kind of reassurance.

Joe kissed the top of her head, hugging her a little closer. "Not for a lack of trying," he said, his voice a mere whisper.

Joe left a short time later and Randy ate alone, something she had grown accustomed to. She realized they had just overcome the first of many obstacles standing in their way. She also knew that if she just turned the job down, everything would be fine again. But something inside her told her she had a right to want more out of life, that she had a right to have a job that she loved, not just a husband, or kids or a home. She had seen Midnight have it all, and she knew she could too.

Randy had no idea that Midnight's life wasn't perfect, that she and Rick were having major problems—and that the job wasn't all it was cracked up to be either.

****

The day she was scheduled to leave for Sacramento, Midnight got up at her usual 6:00 a.m., took a shower, and got dressed in clothes that she had become accustomed to but were not really what she considered her style—a business outfit. She wore a straight-cut navy blue skirt—which was admittedly a little shorter than a normal business skirt—a white silk blouse, and, left on the hanger until she needed it for the flight, a navy blue tailored jacket that reached just below her waist. The skirt was belted, but only so she could wear her high-ride holster and her badge; the jacket covered both nicely.

Midnight put on rarely used makeup, just eyeliner, mascara, blush, and the merest hint of color on her lips. She also wore gold-and-pearl earring studs and a thin gold chain with a small pearl-and-gold pendant that Rick had given her the year before for Valentine's Day. Her hair was up in a very casual French twist, strands escaping to fall in lazy curls around her face and neck. Her seemingly year-round tan and copper-gold hair complemented the colors of her suit and gave her an appearance of health and vibrancy.

When Midnight walked into the kitchen, Rick stared at her for a long moment, almost awestruck. Mikeyla, who was sitting in her booster seat, let out a little "Wow," at which Midnight smiled.

"What?" she asked self-consciously, wondering if Rick was going to complain about her dressing up for the trip. He was still mad about it and didn't want her going; they had argued the night before. She had told him she was going and that their discussion was over.

But now Rick sat staring at her like a star-struck kid. He shook his head, his eyes never leaving her face. "You look... incredible."

"Thanks," Midnight said, embarrassed. She never did know how to take a direct compliment, especially the way things were between her and Rick.

Since the night Deborah left and Rick stayed out until three in the morning, they had barely spoken to each other except to argue. Midnight had refused to ask where he had been, assuming correctly that he'd been with Sheila. Rick had not mentioned it at all, not feeling the need to explain himself to her and aware that bringing the night up would indicate some guilt on his part—of which he had plenty, but he refused to recognize it. Sheila had been all over him at the club and had insinuated that she'd be amiable to a reconciliation between them. Rick had responded to her hints with his usual wit, but had declined to actually act on any of them. Sheila and he had danced a few times, and she had clung to his side most of the night, reminding Rick of his gang days when girls would actually get into fights about who was going home with him that night. The thought had struck him when he was sitting in the club with Sheila giving every other woman inside their group and out the look that said "Hands off." Rick found himself enjoying being the center of a woman's attention again, and had fleetingly thought about actually doing something with Sheila. Certainly, she was an attractive woman; she was a bit on the overdone side, Rick reflected, automatically comparing her to Midnight, but all the same, at least she paid attention to him and didn't put anything before him.

Now, looking at Midnight and seeing how beautiful his wife really was, he found himself glad that he had not done anything serious with Sheila. Realizing he was glad about his fidelity actually made him angry. He had a right to be happy, didn't he? What was he—a coward? He didn't like the idea one bit. He also didn't like his current train of thought, so he tamped down on it and concentrated on Midnight as she poured herself a cup of coffee. She sat down at the table, picked up the newspaper, and began to read.

Midnight found herself a little angry at Rick's compliment. *If I look so incredible, why does he have to go out with Sheila?* A few minutes later, she finished her coffee and stood up, looking pointedly at Rick.

"Are you driving me to the airport later, or should I ask Joe?" she asked.

Rick tensed at the mention of his best friend's name. Midnight knew it irritated him that she was still so close to Joe, and that if he refused to do something—like take her to the airport—she could easily pick up the phone and get Joe to drop whatever he was doing and come to her rescue. Rick was still supremely pissed about the night of the party when Midnight had called Joe to pick her up. He had hoped she would have to come back and ask him for the keys or to at least drive her home—then he would have had the upper hand. As it turned out, she had, as usual, come away ahead of him, and had proven once more how little she needed him or relied on him.

"Yeah," Rick said irritably. "I'll drive you. Joe's got his own problems."

"And they are?" Midnight said with the merest hint of annoyance.

"You know, with Randy thinkin' she's cop material and all," Rick said triumphantly.

"Well, I guess you'll just be one more male chauvinist pig with egg on his face when she makes it through, now, won't you," Midnight replied pertly. With that, she bent down to her daughter, ignoring Rick's glower. "How 'bout a kiss, little one?" Mikeyla immediately threw her arms around her mother's neck and gave her a resounding kiss on the cheek.

"When are you coming back?" Mikeyla asked, her little voice slightly teary. *Great*, Midnight thought, *something else for Rick to hold against me*. Of course, Midnight knew, as did Rick, that Mikeyla would ask her almost the same question on a daily basis, not wanting Midnight to ever leave the house without her.

"Mommy will be back in about five days. Can you count to five?" Midnight asked, trying to distract her daughter enough to forget how long five days was for her.

Mikeyla nodded, her eyes wide, then held up her hand and raised each finger as she counted. "One, two, three, four, five!" she sang out.

Midnight clapped. "What a smart girl my baby is!"

"Yeah!" Mikeyla said, clapping as well.

Midnight reached down and hugged her daughter one more time. She knew she would miss her, and the thought of it almost made her cry. Midnight had never figured herself for the emotional type about her child, but wonders never did cease.

She turned and walked out of the kitchen, saying to Rick, who was still simmering over her last comment to him, "I'll wait for you in the car."

Rick stared at the space where she'd been, feeling very impotent. He knew he was trying to make her mad about the Randy thing, and was aware that it had backfired. He sighed, standing up and looking down at their daughter, who was watching him now with interest.

"Please don't grow up to be a sarcastic woman like your mother," he said, smiling.

"I won't," Mikeyla replied, sounding very sincere as she smiled up at her father. He winked at her, happy to have one female in the house who agreed with him most of the time.

Marie, the new au pair, came into the kitchen. She smiled at Rick. "Ms. Chevalier let me in."

Rick looked at the woman pointedly. "It's Mrs. Debenshire, if you don't mind. She is married, you know."

Marie looked perplexed, then lowered her eyes and muttered, "Yes, sir." Rick walked out of the room without saying another word.

Marie and Mikeyla watched him go, then Marie looked at the little girl and shrugged. Mikeyla giggled at the face her nanny made. Marie Sophield was English, and she had worked in many aristocratic homes in London before moving to America. She thought it a great coup that she had managed to get a job with an English transplant from London society, and had expected to be working for the same type of people she'd always worked for. She had been pleasantly surprised to find that Midnight was not English, nor did she put on any type of airs, even though her husband's family was considered high society. Mikeyla was an angel as far as Marie was concerned, nothing like the spoiled imps she'd taken care of before. The little girl was agreeable and happy for the most part, enjoying a lot of her parents' love and attention—up until recently.

Marie had only worked for the family for a week, but she could see the tension between Mrs. Debenshire and Mr. Debenshire, and she could see that tension affecting little Mikeyla. Marie intended to talk to Ms. Chevalier—or rather, Mrs. Debenshire—about the little girl's worries when the lady of the house returned from her trip. Mr. Debenshire perplexed her, though. He seemed to be warring with two different personalities. One was the type Marie was used to, the spoiled rich boy with nothing to do but play and order people like her around, while the other seemed very nice and down to earth, easygoing and very much in love with his wife and enchanted with his daughter. Marie didn't know what had caused the Debenshires to become so distant, but she hoped they would be able to work things out.

Midnight sat in Rick's Mustang, looking out the window at the ocean. She knew bringing up Joe had made Rick mad, but she also knew that if she relied on Rick to get her to the airport without a lot of hassle, she would most likely miss her plane.

Rick glanced over at his wife, noticing again how nice she looked and thinking that maybe she looked too good. Here she was flying off to Sacramento to meet with a group of men, and she looked fantastic. Rick trusted Midnight for the most part, but he did not trust other cops or Midnight's desire to avoid entanglements. He knew that many times she'd had to resort to her feminine wiles, usually held in check, to get the results she wanted from these types of meetings. She was going to Sacramento to speak with the heads of two state-level bureaus and possibly even the Attorney General himself about getting some local air and surveillance support from the two units. He knew it was important to her, and that she would give her right arm to receive the support she needed—but just how far would she go, given incentive? Rick didn't know, and he didn't like that. Compounding his concern was the fact that she looked really good all dressed up and made up.

Well, Rick thought, *at least she has a wedding ring on.* He glanced at her left hand and noticed it was bare. He all but slammed on the brakes, and pulled over to the side of the road. Midnight made a small exclamation as she put one hand on the dashboard to brace herself. Not knowing what was happening, she automatically moved the other to her holstered weapon.

Rick looked at her, his eyes narrowed. Midnight recovered her composure after a quick scan in front of and behind them showed everything was clear. Then she turned her attention to her husband and saw the look on his face.

"Now what?" She sighed, unconsciously leaning back against the door, moving ever so slightly out of Rick's reach. He noted the movement and misunderstood its purpose, assuming she knew what he was reacting to.

"Why didn't you at least wait till you got on the plane?" he said.

Midnight looked at him as if he had gone quite mad. "What the hell are you talking about?"

He stared at her for a moment, trying to decide if she was just being evasive, then glanced pointedly at her left hand, still resting on the dashboard. "Forget something?"

Midnight looked at her hand, then back at him. "I guess I did." She shrugged. "Is there some law about having to wear a wedding ring in order to be considered legally married? Wearing one certainly doesn't necessarily keep the wearer honest, now, does it?" Her barb struck home—Rick immediately looked contrite. As she saw his face change, Midnight raised an eyebrow at him, wondering what she didn't know but not willing to ask.

"You can be such a bitch sometimes, can't you?" Rick said. He immediately turned away, his face drawn and angry. A moment later he pulled back onto the road, and they continued the ride in silence.

At the office, a couple of the senior most members of FORS stopped what they were doing and stared at Midnight when she walked in. The whole team regarded Midnight with a high degree of respect, which she worked hard to earn with each of them. One of them, a very large Samoan named Tiny who had a crush on her that went way back, almost tripped over himself when he walked by. He, too, stopped and stared at her.

"Alright, guys," Midnight said, holding up one hand in a stop gesture. "Nothin' to see here, show's over, go on about your business," she recited, like a street cop at a crime scene. A mild chuckle made its way through the room as Midnight walked to her office. Rick started toward his cubicle but was stopped by Spider, who had been with FORS from almost the beginning.

"You're lettin' her go out of town lookin' like that?" Spider asked, elbowing Rick companionably.

Rick looked at the other man for a moment. He knew he was joking, but it still bothered him that his wife received such attention from other men. Finally he sighed dramatically. "Do I have a choice?"

Spider laughed, shaking his head. "Not likely." He cuffed Rick on the shoulder before walking away. "Later, man."

Rick sat down at his desk and looked at the paperwork there. He was working on a case with a new member of FORS, a young Mexican man who was still in the chip-on-the-shoulder phase, always trying to prove how "bad" he was. Rick liked the kid, but he knew there was going to come a time when the youth would have to face the music and realize that being the number one gangster wasn't all it was cracked up to be. His name was Manuel—everyone called him Manny. Just as Rick was wondering where Manny was, in he walked. The kid had a knack for showing up at just the right time.

"Hey, gringo," Manny said. His tone was friendly, his Mexican accent purposely thick. He leaned against Rick's desk. "Midnight es muy caliente today, eh?" he said, shaking his hand as if it had been burned. He eyed Rick carefully, waiting for his reaction.

Rick didn't fail him, scowling at the younger man. "Back off, Manny," he said, low and threatening. It wasn't that Rick thought

Manny would make any sort of play for Midnight, and even if the kid did, Midnight would just laugh; at seventeen, Manny was about thirteen years her junior. But Manny knew Rick hated guys drooling and making sexual comments about her, which was why he had done it.

"Hey, man," Manny said, leering, enjoying the game he was playing. "I can't help it, she's smokin'."

Rick nodded tightly. "Yeah, she is—and she's mine, so drop it." It was not a request; it was a barely veiled threat, and Manny took the cue to back off. It wasn't that he was afraid of the Englishman, he told himself, but he had to work with the guy if he was staying in the unit.

Manny shrugged, holding up his hands defensively. "Okay, man. Jeez, can't a homeboy mess with you?"

"Not today," Rick said simply.

Manny and Rick worked through most of the morning, collating what they knew about a gang called the B Boys. Before Rick knew it, Midnight was standing at the entry to his cubicle. He looked at her, then at his watch.

"Shit," he muttered. They should have left about fifteen minutes ago. "I gotta go for a while, Manny." He stood and pulled his jean jacket off the back of his chair, sliding his gun in the shoulder holster and verifying that he had his badge clipped to his belt. "I'll be back," he said, then held out his hand to Midnight in a "you first" gesture.

Midnight led, walking by Joe's office. She stuck her head inside and saw that Joe was on the phone. He looked up at her, rolling his eyes to indicate the person he was talking to was driving him crazy.

"Call me if you need me," she said. Joe nodded.

Midnight continued toward the elevators, getting stopped a couple of times along the way to sign this or that. Eventually they made it down and out of the building. Once outside, it was obvious a storm was on its way. The clouds had moved in and the breeze was kicking up. Midnight found herself shivering as they walked into the parking garage. Rick automatically took off his jacket and put it over her shoulders. She slipped her arms in the sleeves as Rick put his arm around her, pulling her close. Midnight could smell his cologne, and realized how good it felt to have him so close again.

In the car, Rick and Midnight reached for the heater at the same time, and both laughed. Midnight gave way and let him turn the unit on. When their hands had touched, Rick had noticed how cold hers was, so once the heater was on he reached over and took her hand in his. They drove to the airport in an almost companionable silence. Once parked in the short-term lot, Rick turned to his wife.

"Night," he began, "don't go to Sacramento. Call them and cancel. Tell them whatever, just don't go." She started to shake her head, and he rushed on. "We could go somewhere, maybe a vacation or something. Maybe Hawaii, like Joe and Randy, maybe somewhere else. Just, please, don't go…" He trailed off as he saw the glistening of tears in her eyes. He thought at first she was going to cry, but then he noticed the set to her jaw and realized she was mad.

"Goddamn it," she said, her voice a mixture of hurt and anger. "You have to do this now, don't you? You wouldn't talk to me for a whole week and a half, but now that I'm leaving you want to beg me to stay. It's bullshit, Rick. I can't play these games with you."

"What games?" Rick replied angrily.

"This bullshit with staying out half the goddamned night and coming home half-crocked, and you don't even have the decency to fucking apologize. And now this?"

"What, this?" Rick said harshly. "I asked you to stay here with me and your daughter, and I'd say it takes a pretty screwed-up person to try to turn it around on me."

Midnight looked at him for a long moment, shaking her head almost sadly. "And I'd say it takes a pretty screwed-up person to use a child and what you call love as a weapon." She got out of the car and used her keys to open the trunk, pulling out her small valise and garment bag as well as a leather satchel-type briefcase. She still didn't carry a purse—she never had.

Rick sat in the car, fuming over what she had said. Slamming the trunk, Midnight turned and walked into the terminal without looking back.

Rick stared after her for a few minutes, feeling angry and lost at the same time. He knew what he had done hadn't been fair, but to his way of thinking, if Midnight really wanted to end all the fighting, she wouldn't have gone. He started the engine with a roar and jammed the car into reverse. Cussing under his breath, he drove back to the office.

CHAPTER 6

Midnight walked straight to the airline desk. She pulled her ticket and a letter out of her briefcase and presented them to the woman behind the counter. The woman looked at the ticket and then the letter, then up at Midnight. "Excuse me, ma'am, but what is this, exactly?"

Midnight stared at her for a moment, trying to overcome her irritation at Rick and trying valiantly not to take it out on this obviously inexperienced young woman. "It's what is called a gun letter." Midnight paused to see if she would assimilate that, and when the woman looked at her blankly, Midnight unclipped her badge and showed it to her. "I am a San Diego Police officer, and as a full-time peace officer I am on duty twenty-four hours a day and required to carry my firearm at all times. This letter verifies this information and gives your security office the information about my flights."

The woman glanced at the letter again, then looked at Midnight with renewed respect.

"Okay, ma'am, thank you for explaining that to me. I'll call the security unit and inform them, and I'm sure you'll need to show them the letter." She looked at Midnight for confirmation. Midnight nodded, smiling at her.

"I wouldn't let her on the plane," said a male voice from behind Midnight. She turned and smiled immediately.

"Griff!" she exclaimed as the man grabbed her in a hug.

"How the hell have you been?" he asked, releasing her.

Phil Griffin was a man Midnight had come to see as one of her closest friends. Phil, or Griff, was the Special Agent in Charge of the Bureau of Narcotic Enforcement's San Diego office. She had met him when one of her members solicited BNE's assistance on a case.

"I'm okay," she said, taking her ticket and gun letter from the young lady, who had by now stamped the appropriate sections. Griff moved up to the counter and handed over his own ticket and letter. She looked at the letter, then at Midnight, and smiled. Midnight laughed.

"So where're you headed?" she asked.

"Same place you are," he said slyly.

"What? You're going to Sacramento too?"

"Yep."

"For?"

"For the same meeting you are." His grin widened.

"You jerk!" She punched his arm. "Why didn't you call me?"

Griff shook his head. "Why did my wife divorce me?"

"'Cause you never called!" They'd said the same thing to each other a million times over the last year, since his divorce.

"I really meant to, to see if you had a ride, but obviously you did…" He trailed off as he saw the expression on Midnight's face. "What?"

Midnight shook her head. "I'll tell ya later. We better hurry up, the plane boards in about five minutes." Neither of them noticed the young woman watching them. She was thinking what a handsome couple they made. Griff was a tall, well-built man in his mid-forties. His hair was salt and pepper, and he had a silver mustache and sky blue eyes that twinkled good-naturedly.

Together they hurried to the plane. Since they were allowed to board first because of their law enforcement status, they were able to get seats together. They chatted amiably throughout the hour and twenty minute flight. Griff did not ask her about her ride to the airport, and Midnight didn't really want to get into it.

"So where are you staying?" Griff asked.

"The Clarion," Midnight said. Griff grimaced. "What?" she asked, laughing.

"Oh, nothing, if you like that type of neighborhood..." He trailed off dramatically.

"What's wrong with the neighborhood?"

"Nothing, about twenty years ago."

"Alright, smart ass, whaddya know?" She elbowed him in the ribs.

Griff laughed, shrugging.

The people sitting nearby glanced at them, assuming they were a couple; they seemed to be so close, and getting along so well. The stewardess had her eye on Griff nonetheless.

They continued to chat, deciding that Midnight would drive Griff to their meeting then over to his hotel, the Radisson, and also see if they had any rooms available. With a number of anecdotes, he had managed to demonstrate to her that downtown was still not exactly the safest place in San Diego, even though the Clarion was right across from the governor's mansion.

After they landed, they headed to the luggage carousel. "That's all you brought?" Griff said after securing her bags.

"How much do you think I'll need for a five-day stay?"

"More than that!" He shook his head.

"Jeans don't take up much space, and I only brought one other black-tie outfit."

"Just tell me," Griff said, sounding like an obscene caller, "how many pairs of shoes did you bring?"

Midnight laughed, and put on her breathiest Marilyn Monroe voice. "This pair, and one more."

"Ooooh!" Griff said, shivering.

They broke into laughter, and again, everyone around them noticed.

Once they had retrieved Griff's luggage, they headed outside. A black ninety-seven Maserati pulled up just as they reached the curb. A young man hopped out.

"Lieutenant?" he said.

Midnight smiled and nodded. "How'd you know?"

He smiled shyly. "Well, you look a lot like you sounded on the phone."

Griff burst into laughter. Midnight shoved him, and he laughed harder. "It's true," he said to the blushing youth.

Midnight walked around to the young man, thanking him as he handed her the keys. "Do I need to drop you somewhere?" she asked.

"Much as I'd like that, I get picked up here." He smiled at her again, and Midnight grinned. She glanced at Griff, who was barely containing his laughter.

"And you," Midnight said, pointing dramatically at Griff, "better be good, or I'll leave you here to hitchhike to the AG's office!"

Griff held up his hands in surrender. "Okay, okay!"

"Thanks again," she said to the young man.

"Anytime."

Griff and Midnight—mostly Griff—loaded their luggage into the trunk of the sports car and drove off toward downtown. Griff looked around the car in appreciation.

"Gotta hand it to ya, Night, you sure know how to travel in style. Leather seats, CD player, cell phone, power, everything—probably even a turbo boost for the engine."

Midnight glanced around the vehicle, then shrugged. "Gotta do somethin' with that platinum card they gave me."

"They who?" Griff asked. "And can they get me one too?"

Midnight waved his envy away. "Some credit card company, schmoozing up to Rick to spend his trust fund with their great card."

"Poor baby." Griff clicked his tongue. "Must be rough."

Midnight rolled her eyes. "Oh yeah."

A few minutes later they drove into the parking garage for the Attorney General's new offices. Griff showed his ID at the front guard shack and signed Midnight in. The security officer at the desk handed Midnight a green badge that identified her as a sworn peace officer and gave her access to the entire building. They went up to the thirteenth floor and checked in with the receptionist. A few minutes later an agent came out to meet them.

"Mike Green," he said, shaking Midnight's hand, then reached out to take Griff's as well. He looked back at Midnight. "I'm the Special Agent in Charge at the Sacramento regional office. If you'd come this way, the rest of our group is already here."

Green led them to a nearby conference room, and Midnight assessed him as she followed. She had noted a certain look in the SAC's eyes, one she'd seen many times before. It told her this man didn't have a particularly high opinion of women. Midnight hoped she could change his mind.

Walking into the room, Midnight immediately realized there were a lot more people at this meeting than she had expected.

"I'm sorry," said a handsome older man, who had stood as she entered. "We, ah, ended up with a few other interested parties. Please let me introduce you. First of all, I'm John Davies, Chief of the Bureau of Narcotic Enforcement, and..." He continued around the table, naming each person. There were three police chiefs from local agencies, and two sheriffs as well as an undersheriff. From BNE was the head of their aviation unit—a classic Red Baron type—a Special Agent Supervisor from a local task force, and the Special Agent in Charge of the Violence Suppression unit. There were also two members of the Bureau of Investigation, the chief and his assistant chief. Midnight was the only woman in the whole group, but she was used to that.

The meeting began with Midnight telling the men what her unit was about.

"So you actually employ gang members?" the SAC of the Violence Suppression unit asked.

"Yes, and a lot of times leaders too."

"How do you know that they're straight?" asked the BI chief.

"We check them out, and most of the time we don't recruit anyone we don't know."

"Do you give these people badges?" Mike Green asked, his voice betraying his lack of respect for her accomplishments.

"No," Midnight said, looking the man square in the eye. "I'm a cop, not an idiot." Her stare said, "Unlike you." She caught Griff's eye, and he nodded imperceptibly, his eyes twinkling. "Sometimes," she continued, looking around the table, "I recommend members for the academy, but if they're accepted they go through extensive backgrounds first."

The men nodded, murmuring to each other. Griff raised his eyebrows at Midnight, his lips twisting in a grin.

"So what are you looking for in this?" the VSU SAC asked.

"Well," Midnight said, leaning back in her chair, "I need some local support from your San Diego office, as well as some aviation support from your air wing."

"And what do we get out of the deal?" Mike Green put in, not willing to be one-upped by a woman.

"House on the beach?" Midnight said, keeping a totally straight face. There was silence for a moment, then she smiled and the rest of the room started to laugh. Some of the men even applauded. "Seriously, gentlemen, I can offer you my vast resources of information on your run-of-the-mill gang member, usually leading to a ring of anything from drug dealers to arms salesmen, who usually just happen to be on parole." Her expression was very serious. "Basically covers most of you."

"What about personnel resources?" the BI AC asked.

"I can provide you with some of the best-trained CIs you'll ever need. My people can get you just about any information on any local gang. You can also trust them to handle any buy or reverse you want to try."

Again they all nodded to each other. The door to the conference room opened and the Attorney General himself stepped in. All of the men as well as Midnight stood. He immediately gestured for them to sit down, then walked over to Midnight with an outstretched hand. Midnight shook it.

"I heard we had a celebrity in the building," the AG said, smiling at her.

"Well, I'm not Elvis, but..." She grinned. The AG laughed, and Midnight noted he was a very handsome man, much more so than the last AG, the one that had presented her with her Peace Officer of the Year plaque.

"I hope everything is going well in here," he said, looking around at the men.

Midnight nodded. "I think I've got 'em all fooled." Everyone laughed.

"Trying to boost some of my people again, are you?" the AG asked.

"Just on a part-time basis."

"Well, keep up the good work." The AG shook Midnight's hand again and left. After another half an hour, the meeting broke up.

Midnight was happy to slide behind the wheel of the Maserati again. "Well, that was fun!" she said, taking her jacket off and tossing it over the seat. "Who is Mike Green, anyway? And why does he hate women—or is it just my winning personality he doesn't like?"

Griff shook his head. "No, he just went through a nasty divorce that just about cost him his job, and he's not real fond of the feminine part of the human race at this point."

"Great, lucky me."

"Don't worry about it, I'll set him straight."

"I won't be attending your IA hearing in the near future, I hope."

"Don't worry, Mike and I go way back."

"So did Mussolini and the Italians."

"Funny."

"I thought so."

They arrived at the hotel and checked in, then went off to their separate rooms. Midnight immediately called home, leaving a message with Marie that she had changed hotels and giving her room number. She also told Marie to have Rick call her when he got in.

She undressed and got into the shower. Just when she had rinsed the shampoo out of her hair, she heard the phone ringing. The caller hung up before she could get to it. Assuming it had been Rick, she called home. Marie answered and told Midnight that Rick wasn't home yet, but she had given him the message when he called from his car phone. Midnight thanked her and hung up. She went back to finish her shower.

An hour later she was lying on the bed when the phone rang again. She picked it up.

"Yes."

"Why'd you change hotels?" Rick asked, sounding irritated.

"I'm fine, how are you?" she replied. There was silence on the other end of the line. "I changed hotels because Griff told me that the Clarion was smack in the middle of crime central."

"Griff?" Rick said. "He's there?"

"Yes." Midnight was not in the mood to provide him with any more information. But it wasn't that easy.

"What for?"

"The same thing I'm here for."

"I see," Rick said, his tone changing.

"What is it you think you see, Rick?" Midnight sighed.

"Why didn't you tell me he was going up there?"

"I didn't know."

"Oh, and just what hotel is *Griff* staying in," he asked snidely.

Midnight rolled her eyes. She should have seen this one coming. "Don't start this shit with me, Rick, I'm not in the mood."

"I take it he's in the same hotel then."

"And if he is?" Midnight's growing anger made her sit up.

"You wouldn't be sharing a room to save money now, would you?" He was out and out leering now.

"Fuck you," Midnight said, and promptly hung up. After a minute she picked up the phone and dialed her house. Marie answered again.

"Is Rick home yet?" Midnight asked.

"Not yet, ma'am."

"Thanks," Midnight said, and put the receiver down. "Sonofabitch!" She picked up the television remote from the end table and hurled it at the wall. She stood up and started pacing the room like a caged panther. Her mind was reeling at what she suspected was happening at home. "Shit!" she said, remembering that she hadn't even said hello to her daughter. But she couldn't call now, while she was so irritated. Telling herself that she would call later, she dialed the hotel operator.

"Put me through to Phil Griffin's room, please."

"I'll connect you, thank you."

"Yeah," Griff said a few moments later.

"Where's the nearest bar?"

"My my, aren't we starting early."

"Just shut up and be at my room in twenty minutes."

"Why, Midnight, I didn't know you cared," Griff replied with mock bashfulness.

Midnight sighed. "Cute. Just be here, okay?"

"You got it."

Twenty minutes later, Midnight answered the door to her room wearing her customary jeans and boots. "Let's go," she said, reaching over and pulling her FORS jacket off the chair and leaving Rick's jean jacket behind. She didn't want anything to do with her husband at the moment.

In the car, Midnight put in her *Twister* CD. She had come to really like some of the songs on the album, even though most of it was Joe's type of music—rock. "Long Way Down" came on, and Midnight thought the words basically fit her current mood.

She reached over and turned the song up. Griff was accustomed to her propensity for loud music; he knew it usually meant she was pissed, and now he suspected it had something to do with her husband.

The lyrics blasted out hurt and anger over a damaged relationship, and it was obvious to Griff that Midnight was feeling every one of them. When the last notes died and the next song started, Midnight turned the radio back down.

"Problems?" Griff asked.

"And then some."

An hour and two Long Island Iced Teas later, Griff asked Midnight what was going on.

"What's not going on?" Midnight said sullenly.

"Marriage trouble?" Griff looked pointedly at her left hand. "You are still married, aren't you?"

Midnight nodded.

"I wasn't sure, since you're not wearing your ring…"

"You noticed, huh?" Griff nodded. "Yeah, Rick noticed that too, got into a nasty fight about it this morning on the way to the office."

"What, does he think you're going to come up here and play the swinging single? Doesn't know you very well, does he?"

"That jerk has nerve, thinking something like that about me, considering…" She trailed off, as if she'd lost her train of thought.

"Considering what, Midnight?"

She looked at him, not seeming as tipsy as she had a few minutes before. "Considering the bastard is more than likely cheating on me as we speak."

"No way!" Griff said in disbelief.

"Oh, yes way, Griff. He's seein' some old girlfriend, a society slut."

"What the fuck is wrong with the guy?"

"Got me. I guess I'm just not classy enough for His Majesty, can't take me to high tea or anything."

"Well, if the dumb sonofabitch is fool enough to let you go, just promise me one thing."

"What's that?"

"Promise you'll call me first," Griff said, his face totally serious. Midnight began to laugh all the same.

"I thought you swore off women for at least five years."

"It was seven, and you aren't the garden-variety woman."

"You can say that again," Midnight said, grinning. When Griff opened his mouth to do just that, she said, "Don't do it, or I'll be forced to shoot you!"

They spent the rest of the evening getting a little toasted, and had to pay some passerby to drive them back to the hotel, and then pay for a cab for the guy to get back to the bar. They wound up laughing their heads off at the door to Midnight's room.

"Thanks, Griff," Midnight said. "This was exactly what I needed."

"You aren't going to think that in the morning when old Ace wants to take you up in one of his customized Cessnas."

Midnight immediately looked contrite. "Oh, shit, I forgot all about it. Think a large injection of Dramamine will help?"

"Don't know, but it's worth a try." Griff leaned down and kissed Midnight on the forehead. She looked up at him, her eyes serious. Griff nodded. "You got me, I'd like to prove to you how little you need that jerk you're married to, but I know you better than that, and I know you're a glutton for punishment. Besides, I wouldn't want Sinclair after me. I'll see you in the morning. Oh dark thirty, is it?"

"Oh God, don't remind me!" Midnight said, smiling at her old friend. "It really was like nine, wasn't it?" Her memory was not as clear as it could have been, given her current condition.

Griff nodded, smiling.

"Thank God!" She turned and went into her room. After taking off her clothes, she called the front desk for messages. Rick hadn't called back—or if he had, he hadn't left any messages. Midnight went to the desk and looked at his jacket. Slowly she picked it up and pulled it on. The sleeves were too long; she had rolled them up on the plane. She sniffed the collar, smelling the very familiar scent of her husband.

Still wearing the jacket, she climbed into bed. She snuggled down under the blankets, trying to keep the image of Rick with Sheila out of her mind. Finally she fell asleep, her pillow just slightly damp from her tears. It was something not many people would see, or even believe

110

about the rock-solid lieutenant of FORS. But it was real, and it was her.

The next morning, Midnight showed no signs of the drinking binge. Griff looked terrible, and Midnight let him know it.

"Whoa!" she said, grimacing. "Who dug you up? And what did you do with Phil Griffin?"

Griff looked at her, disgusted. "Shut up. The least you could do is look half as bad as I feel. Any decent person would do at least that!"

Midnight laughed. "Oh, I don't feel a hundred percent, but you can't believe what they can do with makeup these days!"

Griff rolled his head across the passenger seat headrest, leaving his head lolling as he looked up at her. "Think you can do anything for me?"

Midnight pretended to assess him, and finally shook her head sorrowfully. "I think the mortician did all he could, I really do." They were both laughing before she finished her sentence. She started the car and put it in gear.

"Now, where am I going?" she asked. "And don't get me lost!"

"Head down One-sixty and then pick up Fifty going east."

"Okeydokey."

Griff put his hands to his head. "And stop being so goddamned cheerful!"

Twenty-five minutes later, they drove up to BNE's hangar. The head pilot, Tom Dilinger, came out to meet them. "Good morning," he said cheerfully, his smile wide and genuine. He had liked what Midnight had to say the day before—anything that put his planes in higher demand helped his program. Besides, he thought Ms. Chevalier had her shit together, and that was what really counted for him.

Midnight smiled at him. She had liked him in the meeting, thinking he was pretty straightforward and not hung up on the fact that she was a woman. "Good morning," she said as Dilinger opened the car door for her.

"Hey, Phil," Dilinger called.

"Hey, Dil."

"We're waiting on the chief, then we can get under way. You don't get airsick, do ya, Lieutenant?" Dilinger asked.

"It's Midnight, and normally no."

"Normally?" Dilinger looked closer at Griff and started to laugh. "Well that was dumb!"

"Now you tell me," Griff said, inciting more laughter from both Midnight and Dilinger.

The Chief of the Bureau of Narcotic Enforcement drove up. He got out of his car, smiling at the scene before him. Griff was leaning back against the Maserati, his arms wrapped around his stomach, trying to stop laughing. Midnight and Dilinger were all but rolling on the ground. John Davies, who had come up through the ranks and had a pretty good sense of humor of his own, leaned against his car, folding his arms in front of his chest. "Is it something I said?"

The other three officers looked at him, making a supreme effort to stop laughing. Eventually they were successful. "Good morning, Chief," Griff said.

"Obviously," John replied with a grin. He looked at his chief pilot. "Are we set up?"

"Yep, set and ready."

"Good, then let's head up, Lieutenant." The chief gestured for Midnight to precede him. "After you."

"Thank you," Midnight replied.

Ten minutes later, she found herself strapped into the observer seat of a modified Cessna. She was wearing a headset and had a voice-activated mike at her lips. Griff had been very happy to learn there was only room in the plane for three of them.

Utilizing the gyro binoculars, which stabilized the view for the user and compensated for the movement of the aircraft, Midnight got a bird's-eye view of the vehicle playing their "bad guy."

"So this is very effective for counter-surveillance, right?" Midnight said.

"Yep," Dilinger replied. "We can keep our agents from driving into a trap. If the bad guy turns down a dead-end street, or doubles back, we can tell the surveillance team on the ground before they make the mistake of following them. It's also safer for ground pursuits—if our guys lose 'em on the ground, we can still track them from the air. That way our guys don't have to endanger themselves or innocent citizens by running lights or driving at high speeds to catch up to the bad guy. We can stay on them and let the ground crews know where they're at."

Midnight nodded, very impressed with the Bureau's advanced equipment. She was excited about the possible opportunity to use them.

"You use these for search warrants, and raids too?" she asked, thinking about what she could do with such technology.

Dilinger nodded enthusiastically, happy to talk about his program and its capabilities. "Yes. As you can imagine, we catch a lot of strays that way."

"This is great!" Midnight exclaimed.

Later in the day she was given the opportunity to ride in the Bureau's transport aircraft. Again she was impressed with the Bureau's resources and technology. She sat in the copilot's chair, next to Dilinger. Dilinger zealously answered all of her questions about the equipment they had put into the aircraft, and what certain instruments meant and did, obviously happy to brag.

By the end of the day, Midnight was very excited about this aspect of her trip. She had spoken with the chief a number of times, finding John Davies very easy to talk to as well as very intelligent. Chief Davies had told her he would be happy to work with her on some sort of resource sharing, and had given Griff the go-ahead to negotiate this new relationship between the San Diego Police Department and the San Diego Regional Office of the Bureau of Narcotic Enforcement.

That night, arriving back at the hotel after dinner with Griff, Midnight found that Rick had called once. But after thinking about where she suspected he had been the night before, she threw the message away and spent the rest of the evening in her room, watching movies on HBO. The phone rang once, and Midnight decided that if it was Rick, she'd just give him something to think about, so she didn't answer. She knew if it was important he would text her, but she also knew he wouldn't call her if he was with Sheila, because she would not recognize the number and would probably ask about it.

The next day, Midnight went to the range with some of the members of the BNE and the Bureau of Investigations. She was given the opportunity to shoot some of the BNE's weapons, one of which was the Benelli shotgun. Although its kick left a large, nasty-looking bruise on her shoulder, she impressed all of the men with her accuracy. She'd been taught by the best, she told them, her second-in-command—Joe.

That afternoon Midnight very much regretted showing off for the boys. Her shoulder was aching all the way down her arm, so much so that when Griff showed up at her room with Chinese takeout, he suggested she go to the doctor. Midnight shook her head. "I'm okay, just a little sore." To prove she was fine, she reached over with her sore arm to pick up one of the cans of soda he'd brought. She promptly dropped it as pain shot up her arm.

"Oh, yeah, just a little sore, I can tell." Griff said, his face serious. "Don't be dumb, Night. Go to the doctor—maybe you really hurt something."

Midnight rolled her eyes at him. "I've already been dumb," she said, grimacing as she sat back against the pillows. "How d'ya think I got this way?"

After a few more minutes, Griff stood up. "Come on, I'm taking you to the hospital."

After a little bit of arguing, Midnight finally agreed. Griff drove her to Kaiser Hospital and walked her into the urgent care unit. They explained to the triage nurse what had happened, and Midnight was sent for X-rays. Fortunately, since it was a week night, the urgent care unit was not very busy—but they still waited for an hour before they were seen.

The doctor looked at Midnight's shoulder, touching it gingerly. All the while, she stared straight ahead, clenching her teeth and holding Griff's hand with her other hand, flinching only when the doctor tested the range of movement in her arm.

"Well," the doctor said finally, concluding his examination and checking the X-rays, "there is a hairline fracture to your scapula and some serious bruising to the muscle tissue."

Midnight nodded, feeling a little sick from the pain resulting from the doctor's examination.

"I'm going to give you a couple of prescriptions, one for the pain and the other to assist with the inflammation. I would suggest, young lady, that next time, you consider using some padding between you and the butt of the rifle." He wagged a finger at her.

Midnight grinned wanly. "Now you tell me," she muttered.

Griff drove her back to the hotel. By the time they got there, Midnight had decided she wanted to go home. Griff tried to talk her out of it, wanting her to at least get a good night's sleep first—it was already 7:00 p.m. "You'll be lucky to get home by eleven tonight," he said, but Midnight was already shaking her head.

"No, if I'm going to be doped up on painkillers, I want to be that way in my own bed."

Eventually, Griff acquiesced to her decision and told her he'd leave too. "I gotta make sure you get home okay," he said by way of explanation.

After a short flight, Griff made Midnight wait in the terminal while he brought his car around. When a Harbor police officer gave him a hard time about parking in front of the terminal and leaving the vehicle to go in and pick up their luggage—and keep Midnight from even considering grabbing her own luggage off the carousel—Griff flashed the younger man his Special Agent badge and told him that this was official business, that he had an injured San Diego PD officer inside the terminal. It was the truth, after all, Griff reasoned, knowing he shouldn't use his peace officer powers to get away with breaking the rules, but he did need to help Midnight.

By this time, Midnight was exhausted and in visible pain, but she refused to take any of the medication until she got home and made sure everything was as it should be. Griff had told her she was just putting herself through more pain for nothing, but Midnight insisted, explaining that she didn't like how she felt when she took strong painkillers—narcotics. She certainly didn't want to be that way in front of him or any other member of the public. Griff had shaken his head, but gave up trying to convince her.

The ride home, though only twenty minutes, seemed interminable. Midnight leaned her forehead against the window, the cool glass giving her something to focus on. Her head was swimming from the deep throbbing in her shoulder; she couldn't believe how much pain could come from a simple hairline fracture. She'd had more serious injuries, but for some reason this seemed to be worse. Midnight was sure it was just because she was tired—she hadn't slept well the last few weeks. All the tension and anger in the house just seemed to keep building, to a point where she couldn't unwind enough to get a good sleep. Part of her was afraid to take the painkillers, because she knew they would make her tired, and in her exhausted state, she might never wake up.

Reflecting on her morbid thoughts, Midnight knew she was just out of it and that the narcotics wouldn't kill her, but her mind kept churning out possibilities. A few times, her imagination tried to touch on what was happening with Rick, what she might find out when she got home. Would he be there—would Sheila? Had they been there, had they… Midnight recoiled forcefully away from the thought. She didn't want to know, she didn't want to see Rick's face, smug and guilty at the same time. Her thoughts whirled in a tornado of fear, anger, and humiliation, spiraling around in her head, making it tingle with emotions that then shot down to the pit of her stomach, making her want to retch violently. She felt her entire body strain with the effort to remain seated in the car—and just then they pulled up to her house. Midnight grabbed the handle, forgetting about her shoulder in her haste to get out. As she yanked the door open, she gasped involuntarily at the pain that shot up her arm. Then she was on the ground, desperate for air, coughing and crying at the same time.

Griff threw the car into park and jumped out. He ran around the front and skidded to a stop, startled. In the almost four years he had known Midnight, he had never seen her this way. He wasn't sure what to do—he just knew he had to get her into the house. Hopefully that louse of a husband of hers was home. He glanced around, looking for Rick's Mustang—no sight of it.

He rushed to Midnight's side, still reeling at seeing her like this. All he wanted to do was make her pain stop, but at this point he wasn't even sure it was just her shoulder. He knelt down in front of her.

"Midnight," he said soothingly, "I'm gonna pick you up so I can get you into the house, okay?"

Midnight nodded, not looking up at him. Among all the other emotions she was feeling, a deep shame was prevalent. She couldn't control herself, the tears just kept coming, and she just wanted to crawl into the nearest corner, curl up into a ball, and cry. Throughout her life she had always cried in private, mostly in the shower with the water running down her face. Very few people had ever seen it, much less when she was in a state like this. She felt Griff's powerful arms lift her gently. She winced slightly as the movement jarred her shoulder, but her face was against Griff's chest, so he didn't see.

He carried her to the door, then saw the security keypad. "Honey," he whispered against her hair, "I need you to tell me your security code so I can open the door. I'm a cop—you can trust me." He was relieved when he heard her laugh softly. "Three, three, two, four," she said softly. Then in a slightly stronger voice, "And if my VCR disappears, I know where you work."

Griff laughed out loud, seriously relieved that she was obviously coming out of it. "You got it, babe."

Once in the house, he followed her directions to her and Rick's bedroom. It was obvious Rick was not at home. Griff set her gently on her bed. Turning on the light, he looked her over. Her face was wet from her tears, and he dried them with his handkerchief.

Midnight grinned at him. "I thought only really old guys carried those."

"You're so perceptive," Griff shot back.

Midnight nodded, then started to get up from the bed. Griff blocked her.

"Where do you think you're going?" he asked.

"I want to check on Mikeyla."

"You stay here, I'll do it."

"You don't know where her room is."

"So tell me."

He came back a few minutes later. "She's not here. I saw a note on her door from a Marie that said she left her with Joe, that her aunt was sick."

Midnight nodded, relaxing against the pillows. An hour later, Griff had gotten her comfortable. He had heated up some soup he found in the refrigerator, then made her take her painkillers. She was still very shaky, and Griff did not want her alone in the house. Finally he decided to call Joe, hoping he would know where Rick was. It was almost midnight by this time, so Griff wasn't surprised to wake Joe up.

"Yeah," Joe said groggily.

"Joe, it's Phil Griffin."

"Aren't you chasing drug dealers awfully late?"

"Actually, I'm babysitting."

"I see." Joe was still half asleep. "And this relates to me how?"

"Well, I'm babysitting your partner, because your best friend is an asshole," Griff said angrily.

Joe was silent for a minute. "What happened?" he asked, concern creeping into his voice.

"She'll be fine, she just beat the shit out of herself with a Benelli shotgun. I think it's her heart that's not doin' so well. Do you know where Rick is?"

"Obviously not there," Joe replied, his voice cold. He had a feeling something was going on with Rick. He hadn't seen him since Midnight had left. But he was pretty sure where he'd find him. "I'll hunt him up. Can you stay there awhile?"

"You got it. Thanks, Joe. I knew she could count on you—too bad I can't say the same for her husband."

"Yeah," Joe said, hearing the anger in the other man's voice. He hadn't realized the BNE SAC had such a thing for Midnight, but he wasn't surprised either. He knew how she could make someone want to protect her against everything—he'd been there many times.

Half an hour later, Joe drove up to the Thelands' home. He was not surprised to see Rick's Mustang parked out front. Fortunately—for everyone involved—Sheila and Rick were still in the car. Had they been in the house, Joe would have woken everybody inside in order to drag Rick out of there. As it was, he had to fight not to knock out the man he considered one of his best friends in the world. The problem was, Midnight was the other person he considered his best friend in the world.

Joe walked over to the driver's side of the car and snatched the door open. To his surprise, Rick and Sheila were only talking. Rick's head snapped around, and out of sheer reflex his hand went for the holstered weapon under his right arm. Joe glared at him; when Rick's hand moved away from the weapon, Joe hauled him out of the vehicle by a handful of his jacket. "Little late for tea, ain't it?" Joe said harshly. Rick's face was only inches from his own.

"What the fuck are you doin' here?" Rick asked, anger his first reaction to Joe's words.

"I came to find you, and it's pretty obvious I needed to." Joe craned his neck around to shoot Sheila a dirty look.

"Joseph Sinclair," Sheila began in her most regal tone.

Joe cut her off. "Save it, bitch! Don't you have nothin' better to do than stealin' another woman's husband?"

Sheila got out of the car and turned as if to leave. "I will not—"

"You better be plannin' on sayin' that you will not see this man again, 'cause anything else comes outta that mouth o' yours an' I may shut it permanently."

Joe had released Rick by then, and Rick was leaning back against the car, staring up at the sky. He knew he was in the wrong place, and in deep.

Sheila, on the other hand, had no idea who she was dealing with, or how loyal Joe was to Midnight and her marriage with Rick. She whirled around, the pillar of society, and stalked around the car. She stared insolently up at Joe.

"Richard is a grown man. He can see who he chooses," she said, her voice that of a queen, not a mistress. "And," she started, and Rick knew what she was going to say—he began shaking his head, but Sheila paid him no mind. "If that uncouth slut he's married to wanted to stay married, well, then she'd stay at home where she belongs, now, wouldn't she?"

Rick had closed his eyes, sure of what Joe's reaction would be. He was very surprised Joe had even let her go past the words "uncouth slut."

Joe stared down at the woman he had known a good portion of his life, having come from the same social circles. He realized he had never wanted to strangle a woman more than he wanted to at that moment, but he controlled himself. He looked at Rick, and Rick was surprised to have Joe's anger turned back on him so quickly.

"Is that what you've told her?" Joe said, cold as an iceberg. "You've told her that Midnight is leavin' you alone? Have you convinced her that Midnight doesn't love you? Or are you tryin' to convince yourself?"

Rick stared at Joe, his mouth set in a hard line. "I tried, Joe," he said finally, anger of his own starting to flood his veins. "I tried to get her to stay, tried to get her to go away with me, but all she gives a shit about is that goddamned job!" He sneered. "And you know what, your little goddess ain't so innocent either. She was shackin' up with some guy up there—she isn't as pure as you'd like to think." Rick looked Joe square in the eye. "And as far as I'm concerned, if you love her so goddamned much, why the fuck didn't you marry her?"

That was the final straw for Joe. His punch hurled Rick a good three feet and laid him out flat. Rick sprawled on the ground, his vision swimming as he stared up at Joe.

"When you're man enough to get up, just try me," Joe said, his voice colder than Rick had ever heard it. "And while you're lyin' there, let me enlighten you a little bit, you dumb sonofabitch. That guy she was 'shackin' up with' is at your house right now, with your wife. He's takin' care of her 'cause you're here with princess. Now," Joe all but shouted, "tell me again how I don't know Midnight. And as far as marryin' her, I would have, but she turned me down a long fuckin' time ago."

Rick said nothing. He had dropped his head back on the pavement and now lay there motionless, gazing up at the sky.

"To hell with ya," Joe said, waving Rick away. "I'll take care of her. You stay here with your tart."

Joe got into his car, kicking up dust and gravel as he accelerated out of the driveway.

Joe got to Midnight and Rick's house five minutes later. He punched in the code to open the door and strode into the bedroom where Midnight lay asleep. Griff was sitting in a chair in the corner, watching her. He looked up when Joe entered. His eyes went to the hallway behind Joe, expecting Rick to be right behind him; he was very surprised when Rick did not appear. He looked at Joe again, closer this time. He could see the anger in Joe's eyes now, and he knew Rick wasn't coming.

"So," Griff said almost in a whisper, "where is he?"

Joe motioned Griff to the hallway, not wanting Midnight to hear what he was going to say, but Midnight's voice stopped them both.

"He's with Sheila, isn't he?" The question was for the most part rhetorical, but the look on Joe's face told her everything she needed to know. She nodded slowly, her eyes closing, but Joe knew she wasn't sleeping again. He knew she was holding back tears she didn't want Griff to see.

"I'll take care of her from here," Joe said to Griff, nodding toward the hallway. The look on his face told Griff he should bow out at this point. Griff looked over at Midnight. She was trembling ever so slightly, and he was pretty sure she was about to repeat the surprising scene from out in the driveway. Griff knew Midnight wouldn't want him to see, and in a way he didn't want to watch her fall apart again—it hurt too much, especially knowing she couldn't share it with him, so he couldn't make everything alright. Griff nodded to Joe and turned to leave. Again, he was stopped by Midnight's voice.

"Griff?" she said quietly. Her eyes were open again, unshed tears shining in them.

"Yeah?" he replied softly.

"Thanks," she said simply. But she looked at him for a long moment, her eyes pleading with him to understand why she needed him to leave just now. Griff nodded and left the room.

Joe moved to sit on the side of the bed, next to his partner of many years. He looked down at her, and knew that the lack of Rick's presence was affecting her deeply. He could see the betrayal in her eyes, and a hurt that she wouldn't acknowledge at this point. Midnight's eyes narrowed as she looked away from Joe. He could tell she was rallying all of her pride, her courage, her ability to overcome anything. He didn't say a word as he watched Midnight go through a battle with herself. She was warring with her emotions; part of her wanted to curl up into a ball and cry, and another part of her wanted to find Rick and Sheila, and one, beat the shit out of Sheila, and two, take her wedding ring and shove it down Rick's throat. Fortunately for her she was stronger than crying like a baby, and Rick and Sheila were equally fortunate that Midnight had some modicum of control left.

After a little while, Joe leaned against the headboard alongside Midnight. She rested her head against his chest and stared unseeingly at the wall while he stroked her hair. Joe was pissed as hell at Rick for what he was putting Midnight through. What irritated him more was that he knew Rick really loved his wife; it was his pride that was causing the problem. He knew Midnight wouldn't give up FORS for Rick, and that Rick wouldn't stand for what he considered coming in second in her life. As far as Joe could tell, there was no easy answer here, and he couldn't do a damn thing about the situation. He really hated that. At the moment, though, Joe did know Rick was in the wrong, and for that reason he was siding with Midnight. If things had been reversed, and Midnight was cheating, Joe would have just as vehemently sided with Rick. So he sat, quietly holding his partner and wondering what would happen. He knew only time would tell.

CHAPTER 7

Rick didn't come home that night, nor the following days. After about three days, Midnight felt up to going back to work. She had spent a lot of time with Mikeyla while she was off. Randy had brought the little girl over the morning after the incident with Rick. Mikeyla was thrilled to see her mother and immediately threw herself into Midnight's arms. Midnight had had to fight back a wave of nausea as Mikeyla bounded into her, but she didn't want the little girl to know she had hurt her mother, so she said nothing.

A few hours later, Midnight explained to Mikeyla that Mommy had an "owy" and that that was the reason she couldn't pick her up. Mikeyla had wanted to see the owy, so Midnight showed her part of the dark bruise on her shoulder. The little girl asked if a "bad guy" had caused the owy, but Midnight told her that Mommy just hadn't been careful at the range. Midnight had spent another ten minutes trying to explain what a range was, and subsequently what a shotgun was. By the time Mikeyla nodded her understanding, Midnight was ready for a nap, and so, thankfully, was Mikeyla. The two lay down together on Mommy's "big girl bed" and slept.

It was almost ten hours before Mikeyla asked about Daddy, assuming he had been at work. When Midnight said Daddy was out of town, Mikeyla asked if he had been with Mommy the previous days. Midnight knew then that Rick hadn't been home the whole time she was gone. Mikeyla said that Daddy had called a lot, but Marie had said he was busy and that was why he wasn't home.

Later that day, Midnight had talked to Marie and the girl had explained that Mr. Debenshire had called from his car the day that Midnight left, and had stopped by the house at one point during the evening, changed clothes, and left again. Marie said she hadn't seen him after that, but she was pretty sure he hadn't come back to the house. She also explained that on the day Midnight was at the range in Sacramento, Marie's aunt had called, telling Marie that she needed her. Marie had tried to contact Rick and had also tried the hotel where Midnight had been staying, but she couldn't get ahold of either of them. Midnight asked what time Marie had called the hotel, and Marie indicated it had been about 6:00 p.m. Midnight realized she had been at the hospital at that point. It dawned on her, with growing anger, that Rick had basically dumped their daughter with Marie and gone off with Sheila and her high-priced friends.

By the time Midnight saw Rick, almost a week after she returned home, she was ready to kill him. Midnight was sitting in her office when she heard his voice. She felt herself tense in anticipation, but he hadn't even come to talk to her. Obviously, he knew she was aware of his indiscretions and didn't want to get into a confrontation with her in public. That's what she thought, anyway, until her door was slammed open and Rick stood there, looking fit to be tied.

"What the fuck is this?" He waved some papers in her direction. They were divorce papers.

Midnight remained calm—a bit surprised that he had been served so soon, but calm all the same. "What does it say?" she asked coldly.

"Don't get smart with me, Midnight, you know goddamned good and well what it says. But you don't actually think you're taking my daughter away from me too?"

"Oh." Midnight steepled her hands in front of her, the picture of confidence. "I don't just think it."

"Like hell!" Rick yelled.

"Do try to get a grip on yourself," Midnight said, glancing at a group of people outside her office who were looking in their direction.

"Oh yeah, I'll get a grip." Rick stepped inside and slammed the door behind him. "If you actually think that you have a right to take Keyla away from me, you've got another think comin'."

"Yes, I do, as a matter of fact," Midnight said, her voice still as cold as ice, "and that thought is that you had better watch your mouth. I'm still the boss at work."

"Yeah, I'm sure you are, but you won't be for long—my boss, that is. I'm requesting a transfer." Rick watched her to see how she'd react. He was trying to hurt her, wanted to wipe that cool look off her face, but he was sure he wouldn't manage it. For all the noise he was making about losing Mikeyla, what he was reeling from was losing Midnight too.

"Approved," Midnight said simply. Then she turned her back on him, went to her computer, pulled up a menu, and selected a document. She tapped out a few sentences then asked over her shoulder, "What section do you want to go to? Vice? Homicide? You name it."

Rick stared at Midnight's back for a long moment, knowing that what he said next could affect him for a long time. He didn't want a transfer, he didn't want a divorce—he wanted his wife back, and nothing else. Midnight waited patiently, her eyes trained on the computer screen. Rick couldn't see the glistening tears in her eyes; she didn't want him to either, and was sincerely hoping she wouldn't have to say anything else, because she knew her voice would belie her feelings.

Rick finally lost all his fight. He turned, opened the door, and walked out, closing the door quietly behind him. Midnight let out her pent-up breath, slumping in her chair. She knew things were going to remain difficult as long as Rick was in the unit, but she really didn't want him to leave either.

Joe wandered into her office about an hour later. He had heard about the scene and wanted to find out what had happened.

"He was served," Midnight answered simply.

"With what?" Joe asked, perplexed.

"Duh." Midnight rolled her eyes. Then, seeing Joe's blank look, she said, "Divorce papers."

Joe's eyes widened. "No shit?"

"Obviously not." Midnight met Joe's stare. He hadn't expected it to happen so soon—he had been sure Rick would come home and grovel enough to get back into Midnight's good graces. But obviously that hadn't happened, and seeing Midnight's face right now, Joe realized that even if Rick had come home, Midnight wouldn't have forgiven him anyway. Joe left her office a while later, feeling very down. It didn't help matters much that Randy had received an academy date that was only three weeks away. Joe was beginning to feel like he was living someone else's miserable life.

****

Things between Joe and Randy had continued to be strained, and now with a start date for the academy, Randy felt like she needed someone to share it with. She had become acquainted with another woman during the testing phase and had kept in touch with her since the backgrounds had started. Sarah Dickerson was the antipode to Randy's fair, petite looks. She had the build of a woman who spent a lot of time in a gym, and she wouldn't be classified as beautiful; her looks were a little on the basic side. She had brown hair, brown eyes, and a sallow skin tone. She did, however, know how to utilize makeup to make her look softer, and how to dress to keep people from being put off by her athlete's build.

Sarah had been very easygoing about the entire process, not feeling the strain of the competition as the other women had due to her confidence in her ability to handle the physical aspects of the job. Randy had confidence in knowing that getting the job as a police officer was not life or death; she had the security of knowing Joe would take care of her, and that went a long way toward projecting self-confidence in herself. Randy had changed a lot in the three years she had been married to Joe. She had gained more assurance in her looks, as well as her ability to handle most any situation. What she didn't realize was that her ability to handle things stemmed from her reliance on Joe as, basically, backup. It was her unrealized dependence on her husband that worried Joe.

Joe didn't feel he could point out to her that she needed him, knowing that would only make her more determined to do this on her own. He was also afraid that her blind, headlong path would lead her into something that could hurt her, but he didn't know how to express his fears to her in a way that wouldn't make him look like an insensitive, egotistical asshole. So he remained silent. And Randy found it necessary to hang out with someone who was supportive, and who wanted what Randy herself thought she wanted—to be a police officer.

Randy called Sarah when she received her academy date, and she was pleased, but not surprised, that Sarah had received the date also. Sarah suggested that they go out and celebrate. Randy had hesitated, having never gone out without Joe, and not sure how Joe would react to this. But then the stronger, willful side of her personality, the one that was newly born, said, "Why shouldn't I go out and celebrate? Joe could come if he wants to." But Randy knew he wouldn't, having already made no secret of the fact that he was not pleased. Randy found herself agreeing and making plans for that evening.

Hanging up the phone, Randy looked toward Joe's office. He was reading a report, leaning back with one booted foot on an open lower desk drawer. *Now*, Randy thought, *how do I tell him?* She figured she'd do it on the way home that evening, but as fate would have it, she didn't have to.

Twenty minutes before they were to leave, Midnight got the word that they had received a search warrant on a gang that Rick and a newer FORS member, Manny, had been tracking. Midnight wanted Joe in on the warrant, and subsequently, Joe had given Randy the keys to his Porsche and told her to be careful on the way home. A few minutes later, Joe, Midnight, Rick, Manny, and Spider left the office, carrying their bulletproof vests and shotguns.

Randy left right after them—actually leaving early, which she rarely did. She arrived home and went in to take a shower. She dressed casually in jeans, a teal cotton shirt, and white high-top tennis shoes. She slipped on a white jean jacket, pinning on a broach with delicately laced gold chains hanging down from a half-carat sapphire. It was a beautiful pin, and she had delicate gold-and-sapphire earrings that dangled in the same way. She let her hair flow loose, much like Midnight wore hers most of the time, and carefully reapplied her makeup, using just a little bit more navy blue eyeliner and mascara than she usually did.

When she looked at herself in the mirror, Randy decided that she looked pretty good. She also felt a flash of guilt that she was trying to look good, and it wasn't for Joe. She put the thought out of her mind, knowing that if she allowed herself to think too much along those lines, she would spoil her time with Sarah. She was secretly excited about the idea of being at a bar without her husband, curious what people would think. Again, the guilt made her stop for a moment. She looked down at the beautiful diamond ring on her left hand and told herself that no man would miss that ring. They'd know she was married, so what did she have to feel guilty about? She left, taking the keys to the white Jaguar that Joe had purchased just for her.

Sliding behind the wheel, Randy felt an incredible rush at doing something her husband knew nothing about. Here she was sitting behind the wheel of a beautiful car, she felt great about the way she looked, and she had the evening to spend partying with a woman whose life was much less fettered by guilt. Starting the car, Randy once again was amazed at the powerful purr of the engine, the almost heady smell of the leather interior. She switched on the radio; Gloria Estefan's version of "Turn the Beat Around" was on the local pop/rock station. Randy turned it up, enjoying the dance beat. She backed out of the garage, and a few minutes later she was driving down Interstate 5. As she passed Mission Bay, the sun was just setting, and the brilliant orange and deep pink of the sun on the scattered clouds and reflecting on the water made Randy feel young and carefree.

Randy drove up to Park Place, remembering when she had been there before with Joe, Midnight, and Rick, and members of the Scorpions had confronted Joe and Midnight in the parking lot. It had been terrifying, and Randy hurried into the club. Sarah was sitting at the bar. She stood as Randy came over to her.

"Let's grab a table," Sarah said. "I want to get close to the band."

Randy looked up at the stage and read the name of the band. "Flyweil?" she said, remembering the name well.

"Yeah, why? Have you heard them?" Sarah asked, surprised. She hadn't thought Randy got out much.

"My, uh, husband knows them."

"Oh, wow, really! I think the lead singer is so gorgeous! Do you think you could introduce me?" Randy had never seen Sarah gush—it was different.

"I don't know if they'll even remember me. I was only here a couple of times, and it's been a while…" Randy trailed off as she saw Sarah looking crestfallen. "But if they do, sure, I'll introduce you, okay?"

Sarah brightened again. "Cool!"

When the waitress came over Randy started to order a soda, but Sarah waved that away. "You gotta try a Fuzzy Navel."

"A what?" Randy asked, laughing.

"No, really, it's great. It's orange juice and peach Schnapps."

Randy thought about it for a moment, then shrugged. "Okay."

Half an hour later, Randy had had three Fuzzy Navels, and she decided she had better switch to coffee or she wouldn't be able to drive home. When the band started to play, Sarah dragged Randy onto the dance floor. The Fuzzy Navels had gone a long way to loosening Randy up; Sarah goaded the rest out of her. Soon they were dancing together, with other women as a group, or with the guys that seemed to swarm around them.

One of the men was paying particular to Sarah, which left Randy on her own a number of times, but she was never at a loss for a partner; guys were asking her to dance left and right. Randy was thrilled with the attention. She was used to Joe being there, and any man who even glanced in her direction twice would receive a dangerous look in return from her husband. The look usually served well enough to discourage any interested men, but if they decided to challenge Joe, they would back down real quick when he stood up, all six foot four inches of him. It helped too that Joe carried himself with all the confidence of a seasoned cop who was also still sometimes a gang leader. Nobody wanted to mess with Joe for long, because one look at him told anyone that he could back up what he was selling.

After the band's first set, Randy and Sarah went back to their table. The guy that Randy had ended up dancing with followed them. He kept asking her questions about herself, what she liked to eat, where she liked to hang out, things that Randy didn't really want to answer for a guy she'd known all of five minutes. She wasn't used to dealing with overzealous men; Joe usually took care of that. Randy was trying to work up the courage to tell him she thought it was time to go back to his friends, who were, she noticed, watching him trying to score. Right before she was going to say something, a familiar voice cut in.

"'Scuse me." It was Steve Tally, Flyweil's bassist, edging the other man out of the way. "Randy!" he exclaimed, then moved to hug her. "How's that really big cop husband of yours?" He emphasized the words, and the other guy got the idea and left in a hurry.

"Steve!" Randy hugged him back. "I didn't know if you'd remember me."

Steve stood back, smiling. "Remember you? Hell, I'm still in love with you." Randy laughed, and Steve looked brokenhearted. "So I guess you're still married then, huh?"

Randy nodded, but didn't say anything about the troubles Joe and she were having.

"So where is the big lug?" Steve asked, looking around.

"He's probably breaking down a door as we speak." Randy looked at her watch, and was surprised to see that it was already nine o'clock. "Or maybe not."

"Well, then..." Steve smiled mischievously. "Have a drink with me."

"Well, I don't know..." Randy replied, her expression very reminiscent of Midnight's favorite hard-to-get, don't-touch-or-you-might-get-burned look.

Steve dropped to his knees dramatically, surprising the people at nearby tables. He reached up and took her hand, like a prince would have in a Shakespeare play. "Dear Lady Randy, please, I beg of you, one drink for the parched."

Randy laughed, having forgotten what a nut Steve was. "Okay, okay," she said finally. "But you'll have to get up off your knees first."

"Done, my lady," Steve said, standing up with a flourish.

****

Earlier in the evening, in a seedy neighborhood in east San Diego, Joe and Midnight waited for the signal from Rick to hit the front door, which he'd give once he and Spider were in place at the back of the house. Manny was holding the battering ram at the ready. It had been a battle to get to this point. Rick had been difficult when he saw that Midnight intended to come along on the warrant. Increasingly so when Joe suggested that he and Midnight cover the front door. "No fucking way!" Rick had all but yelled.

"And why the hell not?" Midnight said, not one to be left out of an argument going on around her.

"I don't think you can cut it at this point," Rick said.

"Obviously you've forgotten one important detail here," Midnight replied, her voice as nasty as his.

"And what is that?"

"That is the fact that I say who goes in and who doesn't, and if you had your head screwed on straight you'd remember that, plus the fact that I've hit a hell of a lot more doors than you ever will." Midnight didn't usually pull rank on people, but she found herself doing it with Rick more and more often. Her lieutenant's bars were like a shield she could use against the humiliation of what Rick was doing, warding off the insecurities and anguish.

"Yeah, but this is my warrant, not yours," Rick said, sounding more like a kid in a sandbox who was thinking of anything he could to be right.

Joe was shaking his head, knowing Rick had just said the wrong thing.

Midnight waited an extra couple of beats before answering, wanting to knock her husband out. "For your information, Officer, every search warrant goes through me, and I sign it. They are, therefore, all my warrants, and unless you want to be doing some serious desk duty for the next ninety days, I'd advise you to get off your high horse and brief us!"

Her voice had become strident at the end; she was growing more and more aware that Rick was going to fight her on everything. That thought made her wonder if she should have made him transfer. She knew she was losing her objectivity where he was concerned, and she didn't like to indulge such excesses in her career.

ick eyed her for a long moment, wondering where this Midnight had come from. He knew he was goading her when he protested her participation in this search warrant, but he hadn't been prepared for the fire she had blown his way. Reflecting on it, as he stood at the back door to the run-down house they were about to serve, Rick realized he did recognize that fire—it just wasn't usually directed at him in anger. He knew it was just such a fire that had gotten her where she was today. It was that fire that had attracted him to her from the very beginning. He remembered their first meeting. Midnight had been in a fight with Joe, and she had gotten a little heated talking about it. Rick wondered how they had gotten so far away from where they had begun, so far off their path together.

But he didn't have a long time for reflection, because Manny gave the signal and he heard the crash as the front door was kicked open. He thought he heard Midnight cry out, then the sound of shots. Rick plunged in the back door, all but running over Manny, who was laying down cover for him. All he could think of was getting to the front of the house, to see what had happened.

On his way he encountered one gang member hiding in a doorway, aiming down the hall toward the front door. Rick launched a kick into the man's head, knocking him to the floor. He slumped, unconscious.

"Night!" Rick yelled, his voice belying his concern.

There were a few anxious moments when all he could hear was glass breaking and shouts. When he got to the front of the house, he looked around frantically for Midnight. She was nowhere to be seen. He saw Joe, wrestling with a large, young black man. Rick leveled his gun at him. "Freeze, or I'll blow your fucking head off."

The man froze in place. Joe twisted around, pulling the young guy's arm with him to hold it behind his back, then looked at Rick.

"Cuffs?" Joe asked, grinning. Rick returned the grin and tossed Joe a set.

"What happened?" Rick asked. He was still concerned, having not seen Midnight yet.

Joe nodded toward the front lawn. Rick walked outside just in time to see Midnight finish cuffing a man one and a half times her size. She was straddling his waist as he lay face down in the dirt. Once the man was secure, Midnight moved off him and sat on the ground, and as Rick watched, she rolled over to lie on her back, staring up at the sky. He heard her say, "I'm getting too fucking old for this shit."

Later, Rick noticed that she was holding her right arm gingerly. He found out while they were doing paperwork that Joe had been first through the door and Midnight had come in right behind him. When the shooting started, Joe's first reaction was to shove Midnight back.

She had slammed into the doorjamb with her sore shoulder—that was when she cried out. As they all sat around the conference room table, Midnight needled Joe about it.

"Oh, yeah, just shove the women and children into the life boats, Captain, don't worry about missing the boat and drowning them. That's okay, speed is the most important thing!" Midnight was laughing by the time she finished her barrage.

Joe rested his head on his folded arms—she could see him smirking. Spider was all but falling out of his chair laughing, and Rick and Manny were grinning widely too.

"Look, I told you I was sorry. Can I help it if you have shit for balance?" Joe said, his voice muffled by his arms.

"Shit for balance?" Midnight said. "I don't think I've ever been accused of that one! Shit for brains, maybe, but no one has ever sunk so low as to criticize my equilibrium."

"Well there you have it," Joe said, standing. Midnight noticed him wince a little bit.

"You okay?" she asked, her voice still light.

Joe nodded. "Yeah, probably just a couple of bruised ribs, nothin' to worry about."

Midnight nodded then too. "Serves you right!" she exclaimed, mockingly offended.

Joe grinned as he pretended to reach for her shoulder. Midnight just laughed.

After much more ribbing and a lot of laughter, they managed to get all of their bad guys booked and their reports written. It was ten thirty by then, and Spider had suggested a stop at the local all-night restaurant for something to eat. "I can't help it," he was saying. "Ever since Tammy got pregnant, I feel the need to eat all the time."

"Great," Midnight replied. "So soon you're going to look like Tiny?"

"Yeah," Joe said, poking Spider in the ribs. "I can just see that! Anyway, I'm just gonna head on home. I'll see ya in the mornin'."

The rest of the group headed out to the parking lot. As Rick reached his car he received a text. Midnight, whose car was parked next to his—originally by design when the spaces were reserved—looked over at him with a raised eyebrow, but she said nothing as she got into her car. Rick noted that she winced a little when she moved her arm. Since the night Joe had found him at Sheila's, Rick had heard how Midnight had banged up her shoulder. It had been difficult for him not to ask her about it all evening, knowing she had hurt it again when they conducted the raid.

Rick was still enraged at the idea that Midnight had actually filed for divorce. She hadn't even given him a chance to explain. The truth was, Rick hadn't slept with Sheila before the night Midnight had come home—he had managed to avoid actually physically cheating on her. He hadn't contradicted Joe that night because he knew he had been mentally and emotionally unfaithful to his wife, and he knew he had been tempted to do otherwise. Rick knew Joe would have seen it as cheating either way, even though Rick felt he had been more than fair with Midnight and was absolutely sure she had been sleeping with Griff. Rick hadn't liked him from the beginning, knowing Griff had had a major crush on Midnight from day one.

Rick knew that Midnight was unhappy, and had fooled himself into thinking she would pour her problems out to Griff, and things would take their natural course. He had conveniently managed to forget that Midnight never "poured"—she would answer direct questions if asked and fill in details if necessary. Had he been thinking reasonably, he'd also have realized that Midnight didn't believe in "cheating." Her logic was, "If I want someone else, I'll leave you and have someone else. I don't need to sneak around." But Rick was not thinking logically; he was rationalizing his own dalliances.

After calling the number on the text, Rick went back into the office. He had been asked to report to evidence, so that was where he headed.

An hour later, Rick found himself at a familiar door—his own. He debated ringing the doorbell, feeling very odd about being at his own house but not being welcome. After a moment, he punched in the security code and walked in. He tried to make a point of making his footfalls loud, wanting to give Midnight some kind of warning that he was in the house without having to ask her permission to be there.

Rick did know his wife well. When he walked into the bedroom, she was lying on the bed. The room was dark except for the light from the television. It bothered him to notice that she was wearing one of his shirts, open just above the curve of her breasts. She was lazily flipping through the channels; it was obvious she was very relaxed. She caught the movement in the hallway, and when Rick stepped into the doorway, he noted the quick movement of her hand toward her firearm, lying within arm's reach on the nightstand. Her fluid motion was quickly aborted as she realized who it was. Rick still marveled at her split-second reactions; they had saved her life many times, he knew.

Now, cat-like green eyes watched him closely, as if she expected him to attack her. Then they flicked back to the television, as if dismissing him. "Gotta get that code changed," she muttered. "Never know what could walk in."

"Nice," Rick said, slightly taken aback by her indirect insult. He had felt close to her earlier that evening, as the group ribbed each other and laughed, but obviously her good nature did not extend to him.

Midnight looked at him again, as if surprised he was still there, then sighed loudly. "What do you want?"

Rick leaned casually against the doorjamb, grinning. "You have always had a way with words."

"Yeah," Midnight said, sitting up, sounding a little more irritated this time. "And you're about to hear a number of my better ones. Spit it out, then get out." Her tone held a threat that he knew he'd be wise not to ignore, but he couldn't keep himself from taunting her.

He walked into the room and sat on the edge of the bed, his demeanor very casual. "You are such a charmer, ya know?"

"Yeah, so's my Beretta. What is it you think you want, Rick?"

Rick looked at her, trying to determine what she had meant by her question. He thought he'd heard just a slight lightening of her tone. "Well," he said, a sardonic grin on his face, "since you asked so sweetly, I'll tell ya." He reached into his pocket, pulled out two sheets of paper, and handed them to her. "I need your Jane Hancock on these evidence receipts."

Rick was very surprised when she looked him straight in the eye. Her stare held no contempt, only questions—questions he knew she wouldn't ask. Then she lowered her eyes to the papers, and Rick felt a sudden sense of loss, feeling like they had been very close to making some kind of connection. Midnight reached for the sheets, her fingers touching his for a brief moment. Rick grabbed the moment and tried to hold her hand.

Midnight's reaction was to yank her hand away, setting her off balance, which prompted Rick to reach out to grab her. His hand closed around her forearm. She again tried to escape his grasp, and he ended up with a handful of her shirt, which exposed the dark purple bruise on her injured shoulder. Midnight lay back against the head-board, watching him, her eyes narrowed, but Rick's eyes were on her shoulder. Midnight could read the concern on his face, and it made her mad. Where the hell had he been the night she came home, looking much worse?

Midnight reached her other hand out to snatch the handful of shirt he was holding, but his hand caught hers easily. He held on with just enough strength to keep her from getting it back, and he was staring into her eyes now.

He shook his head slowly. "Night…" His voice was the merest whisper. Releasing her shirt, he gently touched the bruise.

Midnight flinched as he made contact. He glanced at her to see if he'd hurt her; she just watched him, her eyes veiled.

It wasn't pain that had made her flinch, it was his closeness, his touch, his voice—everything she felt for him that she had boarded up behind iron walls came flooding back to her. Her instincts told her to get away from him; every reasoning nerve in her body screamed to run. But she couldn't move. Her heart, and just about every sense she had, made her stay right there. She knew she'd hate herself later, but she just couldn't pull away.

Rick's touch on her shoulder was soft. He too was fighting his emotions. He had no idea what Midnight was going through; his mind was telling him that he was risking having her do some serious damage to him, if he made the wrong move. But he found himself drawn to her, wanting to touch her, to hold her, and much more that he didn't want to let himself think about. Rick met her stare. He moved his hand to touch her cheek, and she closed her eyes in response, shaking her head slowly. Rick leaned forward then, taking the risk. He kissed her hurt shoulder softly, and when she didn't react he moved his lips to her neck. He thought he felt her tremble under his hands.

Midnight's eyes remained closed as his lips touched her shoulder, then her neck. She trembled as she waited for what she hoped would be next. But nothing happened. She opened her eyes to see that his face was inches away, his eyes staring directly into hers.

In that moment Rick saw what she didn't want him to see, and without any more hesitation, he took her gently into his arms, kissing her lips with a passion that was exquisitely familiar. And Midnight found herself throwing her usual caution to the wind. *To hell with it*, she thought.

Their bodies remembered everything they had tried to forget, and they found themselves swept along with the current of their passion for each other. For a short time, all of their anger, fear, rejection, and toils were forgotten. But the time was all too short.

A little while later, lying in Rick's arms, Midnight started to realize how stupid she had been. How easily swayed she'd been by her body's desires. The thought irritated her to no end. As if he had felt her tense, Rick's arm tightened slightly at her waist, as if trying to keep her from thinking the thoughts he knew were going through her mind at that moment. She sensed him shaking his head, and she heard his breath expelled in a frustrated sigh. "Shit," he muttered.

Midnight didn't look at him. "This doesn't change anything, does it?"

Rick didn't respond for a moment. "Don't," he said, his voice soft. "Don't say that. Can't we just enjoy this for a while?" He was pleading, and Midnight knew she wanted to do the same. She nodded slowly, resting her head against is chest. A little while later they were asleep.

Rick woke when he felt Midnight's body tensing. Her head moved against his chest, as if she were shaking it. Her hands were clenched, her breathing uneven. He knew she was dreaming, and he knew what she was dreaming about. "Night!" he said, shaking her gently, mindful of her sore shoulder. "Wake up!"

Midnight woke with a start. She sat up, wrapping her arms around herself in a protective gesture. Rick sat up and put his arms around her shoulders, pulling her back against him. He felt her relax slightly.

"When did these start again?" he asked, concerned. She'd had these nightmares after she was abducted by the Scorpions years before.

Midnight was shaking her head, as if trying to shake the images out.

"Night, it's okay, they're gone. It's over, they can't hurt you anymore. I'm here, it's okay," he said, striving to comfort her. He felt her stiffen suddenly. Then she raised her head, looking at him. Her expression told him what she was thinking.

"But you're not, are you?" she said, her voice cold and dead. She lay down then, moving away and turning her back on him. He knew that what they had briefly rekindled had died again, and he felt it deep in the pit of his stomach. He knew that he'd just lost her again.

****

As Joe drove up to his house, he noticed that Randy's car wasn't in the garage. He wondered where she'd gone. He had sensed earlier that she was nervous about telling him something. She'd seemed on edge, and he knew she tended to act that way when her emerging independent self warred with her old, shy, dependent self. Once inside, he glanced at the refrigerator door, hoping she would have at least left a note. She hadn't. He tried to hold down his growing anger—he didn't want to jump to conclusions.

He grabbed a beer out of the refrigerator and walked into their room. He removed his jacket and his shoulder holster, again glancing around for some sort of note as he tossed both on the chair. Taking off his shirt, he examined his ribs, and did indeed note a dark bruise beginning to color. After a few minutes he decided to take a shower, thinking Randy would turn up by the time he'd finished. An hour later he sat on the couch with the television on, his fourth beer in hand. Randy still wasn't home. He was beginning to feel the pangs of worry, but he kept telling himself she was just out, wanting to make a point of her independence.

Finally, at midnight, Joe flipped off the television and walked back to the bedroom. By this time he was royally pissed, a little bit drunk, and very uncomfortable with the growing ache in his ribs. It was not a good combination for him. Knowing he was likely to tear into Randy the minute she walked in, not the tact he wanted to take with this new defiance of his solicitousness, Joe forced himself to go to bed.

After almost an hour of tossing and turning he got up, frustrated and angry. Throwing on a shirt, he walked out onto the deck overlooking the ocean. He stood holding onto the railing, staring unseeingly at the waves, as a cold wind blew his dirty-blond mane back from his face. A few minutes later, he sat down on one of the Adirondack chairs, his long legs stretched out in front of him. His gaze surveyed the crashing waves, his mind miles away. Even though he only wore sweatpants and a T-shirt, he didn't even notice the cold. He had even left the French doors that opened inward from the deck wide open. By the time Randy found him an hour and a half later, Joe may as well have turned to stone, his anger was so fierce.

Randy walked out onto the deck, having noticed the doors open. She saw Joe sitting on one of the chairs, and she could tell by the look on his face that he was beyond mad. Her first instinct was to lie, to say she'd had a flat tire or something, anything but that she had just stayed out drinking and having a good time. But she knew she couldn't claim car trouble, since her car was still at Park Place—she'd had to take a cab home due to her state of inebriation.

As she stood there, trying to think of something to say that wouldn't make her sound like a naughty schoolgirl, Joe lifted his head to look at her. His eyes were pure ice. Randy was shocked. She knew Joe could intimidate even the hardiest of souls with a look, but she had never had that look turned on her. Every ounce of self-confidence and bravado left her instantly. She was almost afraid of what he'd do; part of her even wondered if he'd hit her. The surety of his upbringing, barring him from striking a woman, suddenly didn't seem so reassuring.

Joe stared at her for a full minute, his eyes taking in the high color to her cheeks and the way she seemed to shrink from him guiltily. When he stood up, her eyes grew wide, the intimidation she felt clear in them. Joe knew what she was thinking, and part of him felt a twinge of satisfaction that she at least realized he did have some power over her actions, and knowing that she hadn't become so independent as to think she could do something as outrageous as this without some sort of repercussion. With his eyes still on hers, Joe walked toward her— and, to her surprise and relief, past her into the house. He went into their bedroom, closing the door quietly behind him.

Randy found it necessary to sit down. She walked into the living room, closing the French doors, then moved to the couch and sat down. She knew Joe probably better than just about anyone, except perhaps for Midnight, and she knew his cold silence was much worse than his fiery temper. The cold came long after the heat of his anger passed. She wondered idly if this had been a major, pivotal mistake. But what right did he have to expect her to stay home? The dutiful wife, Randy thought angrily. She was supposed to cook, clean, and wait patiently for her husband to come home. She spent the rest of the night in the living room, telling herself she didn't want Joe to think he'd won because she crawled into bed obediently. In truth, she was afraid that he might tell her to get out, or something equally irrevocable.

The following morning, Randy woke to the sounds of Joe moving around in the kitchen. She could smell coffee brewing. After a few moments of indecision, she got up off the couch and went into the guest bathroom. She didn't want to run into him just yet. She knew she looked awful. She still had her clothes on from the night before.

Randy found Joe a half hour later in the kitchen, leaning against the counter, drinking coffee. He was dressed all in black, his brown leather shoulder holster in place. Randy thought off-handedly how good he looked in all black, but she knew she couldn't say or do anything to show him that she thought so. Normally she would have said something to him, or gone over to him and removed the coffee from his hand, replacing it with herself. She did indeed realize how incredible handsome her husband was, but at the moment she felt so at odds with him that his discerning good looks served only to emphasize the undercurrent of anger and the change in their relationship.

Randy had managed to shower, dress, and reapply makeup, so she felt confident again in the way she looked. Not like the drunken harlot, she thought sarcastically. She had dressed with care, wanting to prove to Joe that she wasn't cowed by his anger. Her outfit was a little bit more casual than her usual businesslike attire.

Joe watched her over the rim of his coffee cup, but his eyes gave nothing away. At first she said nothing to him, making a point of pouring coffee and sitting at the breakfast nook in the corner of the kitchen. She flipped through the pages of the newspaper, trying to appear unaffected by the oppressive silence. What irritated her the most was that she needed a ride from Joe, either to the office or to Park Place to get her car. *I could call a cab*, she thought idly, but then she realized she didn't have any more cash, having used all but her last dollar on the cab the night before. She supposed she could try to use a credit card, or try to get the cabbie to take her to an ATM, but she knew she would just be making more out of the issue of leaving her car at Park Place than it should have been.

"I, uh," Randy began, not liking the hesitation evident in her voice, or the way Joe turned his head to look at her, as if surprised she had had the nerve to speak to him. "I need a ride," she said, rushing to get the words out.

Joe looked at her knowingly for a long moment. "Where?" he asked. By telling him where she needed to go, she'd be indicating where she had gone the night before, without him having to take the undesirable position of the insecure husband asking his wife where she'd been.

"To work," Randy said, at which Joe raised an eyebrow. He already knew she hadn't driven home. Having noted her condition when she got back, he had checked the garage, ready to crucify her if she had been defiant enough to drive after she'd been drinking. After a moment he nodded, then continued to drink his coffee, letting her squirm a little bit more, not letting on that he knew her car was not in the garage.

Randy watched him for a minute, curious at first why he didn't ask why she needed a ride, when any other time she could have driven herself. Her irritation grew as she came to the conclusion that he did know why, but he wanted her to admit to it, and he was waiting patiently for that admission. *Well*, she thought, *I won't give him the satisfaction.* So she said nothing, hoping he would be curious enough to pursue the matter. He didn't. He waited.

The drive to the office was devoid of conversation, but in contrast to his resigned silence he opened doors for her, as was his customary polite behavior. Once at the office, they went their separate ways.

Later in the day, Randy stuck her head into Midnight's room. "Do you have a minute?" she asked. Midnight looked up from the paperwork on her desk, a pen between her teeth. She nodded, then motioned for Randy to come in and shut the door.

"What's up?" Midnight asked, having noticed the tension between Randy and Joe and worked out that something new had happened.

"I need to ask a favor," Randy began hesitantly. After all, Midnight was her boss, even if Joe and Midnight were best friends.

"Yeah?" Midnight nodded.

"I need a ride." She hesitated again, then hurried on. "I mean, I need to pick up my car, at Park Place." Randy bit her lip, not sure what Midnight would think or say.

"And your car's at Park Place because…?"

"Well, I went there last night, you know, to celebrate my start date for the academy." Randy told the rest of the story, seemingly all in the same breath. "And I sort of drank a little too much, and I didn't want to drive, so I called a cab, and…" Again she hesitated, not knowing where Midnight's loyalties would lie in terms of her fight with Joe, but decided to finish with, "Well, Joe's mad at me for going out, and I don't want to ask him to take me… and so I was kind of hoping that maybe you could?"

Midnight was staring at Randy wide-eyed, as if she couldn't believe her. Randy was sure Midnight was surprised about the drinking and that she'd be mad about her going out without Joe. She began to wish she hadn't asked. But Midnight surprised her by saying, "You took a cab from all the way in Kearny Mesa to La Jolla? Shit! That must have cost a fortune!"

Randy started laughing. She was so relieved that Midnight wasn't mad at her; she was afraid she had made a big mistake asking Midnight to basically go around Joe.

Randy still didn't quite understand her husband's relationship with his partner and boss. Many times when Randy was sure Midnight would side with Joe on something, she found that Midnight would actually fight him. They always argued, but they always stayed friends. Midnight always had her own opinion, like about Randy's career decision—Joe abhorred the idea, and Midnight thought it was great, and she wasn't silent or clandestine about her support of Randy. Randy hoped that someday she could be more like Midnight, not afraid to say what she thought and willing to go the distance to prove it, or have it proven to her that she was wrong. Midnight was almost always willing to accept things and admit that she was wrong—almost always.

Randy left Midnight's office a few minutes later, feeling like she had won a minor battle against Joe, although she wondered belatedly if Midnight would tell him that she was taking her to her car. Oh well, he was bound to find out anyway.

When Joe saw them leaving together, he surmised that Randy had asked Midnight to take her to get her car. It irritated him, but he did have to give his wife credit—she was learning to circumvent him. He was fairly sure that Midnight wouldn't tell him anything either, knowing that Midnight supported Randy's fledgling independence. Besides which, she didn't play that way. If Joe wanted to know something as ludicrous as where Randy had gone, he should ask her.

Later, Midnight would agree with Joe, however, that the least Randy could have done was leave a note to explain she had gone out with some friends, considering she'd never done it before.

In Midnight's Corvette, Randy sat looking at her boss, the woman who had been nice enough to hire a very shy kid to work for people as dynamic and complex as she and Joe were. Randy thought often of the "interview" she had had with Midnight. She had thought Midnight was just one of the team when she sat down next to her that day. Midnight had talked to her, telling her about FORS and asking her casual questions. Clad in jeans, boots, and a cotton shirt, Midnight had put Randy at ease.

Midnight had not treated Randy as a subordinate from the very first day; Midnight didn't treat anyone like a subordinate unless absolutely necessary. Randy respected that. She knew Midnight Chevalier-Debenshire had quite a lot of power and clout in her field, and it would be easy for her to become drunk with that power, but Midnight remained level-headed and fair.

Randy knew about Rick's "affair" with Sheila Theland. Joe had been sputtering when he called her from his car phone the night he found Rick at the Theland household. Randy knew it must be serious if Joe had actually resorted to knocking Rick down. She still couldn't believe Midnight had actually filed for divorce; she also knew Joe had been surprised at her swift retaliation in the face of Rick's infidelity. The fact that Midnight and Rick's marriage might actually be breaking up shook Randy's confidence in her own marriage. Before she had known about the trouble in the Debenshire household, Randy hadn't even considered that Joe might actually leave her if she went forward with the hiring process for the department. But now, she wasn't so sure.

"Midnight," Randy said.

"Hmm?" Midnight replied, her mind elsewhere, thinking about the night before with Rick.

"Are you and Rick... Well, are you really through?" Randy realized after she'd said it that it really was none of her business, but it was too late to take the words back.

Midnight looked over at her, actually surprised the other woman had asked. Randy seemed to be surprising her often lately. Midnight shrugged, then nodded slowly, realizing that Randy was concerned about the stability of her own marriage.

"Are you and Joe still going at it?" she asked point blank, with no hesitation. Midnight knew that Randy knew Joe almost always told her everything.

Randy blew her breath out in a sigh. "Going at it is a pretty safe term to use."

Midnight nodded. "You should have been prepared for this," she said. Her tone was friendly, but her words stung anyway.

"Well, Jesus Christ!" Randy snapped. "You know I'm not the first woman to apply for the goddamned police department!"

Midnight grinned at the other woman's outburst. "No, but you are the first Mrs. Joseph Sinclair to apply."

"Why does that have to matter?" Randy said stridently.

"It doesn't *have* to matter, it shouldn't matter—but that's all a moot point, honey, because it does matter and will continue to matter to your husband. The question is, how far are you willing to push it?"

Randy looked at Midnight, amazed at how simple she made it. All the thoughts and questions, all the anger and frustration, and Midnight summed it up in a simple statement. She thought about what Midnight had said, then shook her head slowly. "I don't know. Do you think Joe would actually let us break up over this?"

Midnight considered the question for a moment, then nodded slowly. "Yeah, I think he could."

"So what am I supposed to do?" Randy asked, anger creeping into her voice. "Am I just supposed to roll over and play dead?"

Midnight grinned at her. "I guess that depends."

"On what?"

"Two things," Midnight said, holding up two fingers. "One, how much being a cop means to you, and two, how much Joe means to you."

"It's not that easy!"

"I didn't say figuring that out was easy, I just said that it only comes down to those two things. What I say, what anyone else says, doesn't mean shit. Just do what's right for you."

Randy was quiet for a few minutes. Then, "What if I lose him?" she said quietly. Midnight could hear the tears in her voice, and she wished she could assure Randy that it wouldn't come to that, but she couldn't.

"Randy, that's the risk you take." Midnight pulled into the lot at Park Place. She parked next to Randy's white Jaguar and turned off the engine. She turned to Randy, looking into the younger woman's eyes. "If you want your independence, it comes with a price tag," she said seriously, "and that price tag may be as high as losing Joe. But this is the real world, Randy, and no one is going to make you any promises. You have to roll the dice and take your chances just like the rest of us."

Randy looked at Midnight for a long moment, surprised at how angry she felt at the other woman's words. "Why doesn't that apply to everyone?"

"It does," Midnight said matter-of-factly.

"What about you? You have everything, a husband, a career, a child. Why can't it be that way for me?" Randy sounded almost childlike, as if she were asking why she didn't get the dolly that laughed instead of the one that wet its pants.

Midnight laughed. "Oh yeah, I have it all!" she said harshly. "A husband who's cheating on me, a career that gives me heartburn, indigestion, and high blood pressure." She pointed an accusing finger at Randy. "You don't think I've given up anything for my career? Or my life?"

"What? What have you had to give up?" Randy asked, knowing she was almost being rude, but fighting for some kind of assurance.

"You want me to be brutally honest here?"

Randy hesitated for a moment, then nodded slowly.

"First, I lost my childhood on parents who should never have had kids, then I lost a little bit more when I joined a gang and had to be tough all the time. Then I lost the only person I loved more than myself, when my brother was killed. Next came losing some of my freedoms by becoming a cop, and putting myself in a place where no matter how hard I worked, some man was going to come along and claim I got my position because I slept with someone, or a whole lot of someones. And worst of all"—Midnight narrowed her eyes, staring right at Randy—"I lost Joe, because I had to choose what was right for me, and I couldn't do the job and be with him. It was that simple."

There was complete silence in the car for a long minute. Randy was surprised that Midnight had put Joe on the list, since to Randy's way of thinking, Midnight was still so close to him. But she realized at that moment how deep Midnight's feelings went for Joe, and it bothered her, because she had the distinct feeling that Joe's feelings for his partner were just as deep. And if he had been willing to let Midnight go… Randy didn't want to think about it. She nodded and muttered a thank you as she blindly reached for the door handle and got out of the car.

Midnight watched Randy go. She knew she had probably said more than she should have, but she wanted the younger woman to realize that life didn't have to be fair, and that things weren't always black and white. Everything was a tradeoff, in some way.

As Midnight drove home, she flipped around the radio stations, stopping at a classic rock station. Kansas' "Play the Game Tonight" was on. She loved the song, and as she listened to the words she realized why. It seemed to be the story of her life, exactly as she had just related it to Randy. Part of her felt guilty for putting all of that on her, but she knew Randy needed a serious reality check. She didn't want the woman going into something thinking everything would work itself out. Midnight reached over and turned the volume up.

The song played on as Midnight drove back toward the beach. She called Marie from the car phone and told the girl she'd be a little late. She was once again very happy she had taken Deborah's advice and gotten the au pair. Marie was keeping Mikeyla's life on an even keel. Midnight felt a stab of guilt, knowing she should be spending more time with her daughter. Promising herself she would, she drove to a spot on the coastline that she loved. It was a rocky cove in the La Jolla Shores area. The waves crashed up to the rocks, and she could sit and watch the seagulls diving for fish. It was a place she liked to go to think. Rick and she had been there a few times together, early on in the relationship. The last year or so had been far too hectic for such reflective moments.

Now, as she sat, watching the sun sink lower in the sky, she thought about Rick, about what had happened between them the night before. She'd avoided thinking about it the whole day. She knew it was only a strong physical attraction that had caused her to lose all sense of reason; what bothered her was that she could still be attracted to him, knowing what she did about Sheila and his betrayal. She had expected her body to be at least indifferent to him, if not repulsed, with the knowledge that he was most likely sleeping with Sheila every night.

But it hadn't, and she'd given in to him so easily, and the lack of control bothered her. She knew Rick was different for her, because her heart was so deeply involved here. She had made a commitment to him, vowed to love and cherish, etcetera, etcetera. But did that mean even when he broke his vows to her? Even when he took her trust and threw it aside like the trash? She'd always deplored women who stayed with men who cheated; she knew that if they had crossed the line once, they'd have no problem crossing it again and again. But she found herself feeling lost and alone, and she hated that feeling.

She had thought that with Rick she had found someone she could be herself with, someone she could love and who would love her, career and all, faults and all. But he'd ended up resenting her career too. He ended up wanting her to give up the one thing in her life that was really important. Somehow the job had become her crusade, her shrine to her brother, and to all the young men and women whose lives ended senselessly in the street, alone. She wanted to build another gang, a gang of people who stood against anyone and everyone—they did it together, with no sudden turns of violence, no requirement for some sort of initiation. She remembered well her violent initiation into the gang so many years before, the fists, the nails, the rings, all of them seeking to hurt her, to test her to see how much she could take. It had been terrifying and violent, and she didn't think anyone should have to go through it. FORS was her way of having the family she'd had with the gang, but without the negative parts of gang life. She couldn't—and wouldn't—give it up, not for Joe and not for Rick. She even wondered if she would be willing to give it up for Mikeyla. She shied away from thinking about it, hoping it would never come to that. She loved her daughter more than she had ever thought possible.

When she was pregnant, she had worried endlessly that she wouldn't feel the things that other women claimed to feel about their babies. She had been afraid that she would see the child as a hindrance to her job. When Mikeyla was born after a very difficult delivery that had almost cost Midnight her own life, Midnight hadn't really felt anything. She looked down at the little girl and told herself that the baby was her daughter, her flesh and blood. But she hadn't felt the extreme rush of love that women claimed to have for their babies the moment they laid eyes on them.

The following weeks were filled with endless feedings, many nights of little or no sleep. It was the only time in Midnight's life when her job had taken a back seat for a while. Midnight had been determined to be a good mother. She hadn't had time then to reflect on whether or not she "loved" her baby; she had just gone on doing what she had to to take care of her. After a couple of months Midnight had gone back to work, and was kept so busy with the two parts of her life she didn't consider the issue.

Then, one morning, Midnight got up after hearing Mikeyla's little noises indicating that she was hungry. Midnight had walked into the little girl's room, bottle in hand. She had looked down at her fussing daughter, and to her utter shock Mikeyla had smiled at her. It wasn't the vague smiles the child had been making over the past couple of weeks, the ones that everyone attributed to "gas." It was a genuine smile. Her baby had looked up at her, recognized her, and smiled at *her*. Midnight had found herself crying in that moment, because suddenly everything had fallen into place—this was what it was about. This little baby depended on her, loved her no matter what her past was, no matter whether she had a career or not. This baby loved her without conditions. It was the most incredible feeling Midnight had ever had. Everyone else in her life had always wanted something from her, everyone else had had conditions. But Mikeyla didn't; she just loved her because she was Mommy.

Thinking about her daughter, Midnight stood from the patch of grass she was sitting on. She got in her car and drove straight home. Once in the driveway, she threw the car into park and all but ran up to the door, throwing it open and calling to her daughter. She heard Mikeyla squeal with delight from the room down the hall, then running feet.

Within moments Mikeyla barreled down on Midnight. Midnight knelt and opened her arms, and the little girl threw herself into them. Midnight stood, whirling her daughter around as Mikeyla laughed and leaned back to watch the walls spin by. After a moment Midnight stopped, feeling a little dizzy but too happy to care. She hugged her daughter close.

Midnight looked up to see Rick standing in the hallway. He was watching them with the most incredible smile on his face. Midnight had to remind herself firmly that she was at odds with him, when her first reaction was to go to him and kiss him deeply for giving her the chance to feel the way she did about her daughter. If Rick hadn't gotten her pregnant she wouldn't have Mikeyla. It was an oversimplified truth, but the truth all the same. As she looked at him now, she could feel her blood pressure soar, her pulse race. His smile lit his face and made her heart pound in her chest.

Rick saw in Midnight, at that moment, the reason he had loved her from the first time he saw her. She looked absolutely radiant as she scooped up their daughter, and Rick couldn't keep from smiling. He had come to the house hoping to talk to her about the night before, wanting to put into perspective for himself what it had meant. He knew his wife well enough to know she had attempted to do the same. Midnight liked to know the bottom line at all costs.

"Daddy came to see you, Mommy," Mikeyla said, sounding very happy about the idea. Midnight realized then that Mikeyla was very much aware of what was going on between her parents, even if she didn't understand the details.

Midnight put Mikeyla down and gestured toward the backyard. Rick followed her out. Midnight sat in one of the wrought-iron chairs on the deck, putting on her sunglasses.

"Don't," Rick said softly, indicating the glasses. "I need to see your eyes."

Midnight looked up at him, surprised that he would make such an unfettered comment, but she put the glasses down on the table in front of her. Rick remained standing, as if he needed to keep moving, to be able to run if he needed to. He stood looking away from her for a few minutes and then, without warning, he turned and stared right into her eyes.

"I need to know," he said, low and serious, "where we stand."

"As compared to what?" Midnight replied cynically.

"Night," Rick began reproachfully, but Midnight held up a hand to stave off his words.

"Okay," she said, shaking her head. "Only one problem. I don't know what you're expecting to hear."

Rick made an impatient noise in the back of his throat as he narrowed his eyes at her. "I'm not expecting to hear anything. I want to know where you feel we stand, what last night meant."

Midnight shook her head, grinning sarcastically. "Gee, and I thought we settled that last night."

"No, we didn't settle it last night. What we settled was that I wasn't here when you needed me anymore. What I'm asking is what you want to do about that."

Midnight stared at him openmouthed. She couldn't believe what he was saying to her. She couldn't believe he actually thought that her need for him could overcome any infidelities he may have committed.

When she spoke again, her voice was strident and tired. "If you're looking for absolution, Rick, go to church. Don't come to me."

She stood up, indicating that for all intents and purposes the conversation was over. She started to walk past him, but his hand whipped out and grabbed her arm—thankfully, not her sore one. Without warning, and with more force than she expected, he pulled her to him and kissed her with all the passion of the night before. When the kiss ended, Rick's eyes were burning into hers.

"Did that feel like a plea for absolution to you?" he asked, his voice as heated as the look in his eyes.

It took Midnight a few moments to find her voice, but when she regained her composure, she pulled her wrist from his grasp. She looked him straight in the eye, and with much more control than she felt, she said, "No, it felt like guilt." She turned and walked into the house, leaving him standing in the yard, watching her go.

CHAPTER 8

Randy's drive home after the talk with Midnight was long. All she could think about was that Joe would be moving out, or doing something equally drastic, when she got home. When she drove up, she saw his car in the garage, in its usual place. Randy knew she was being ridiculous, but she looked inside to make sure there were no boxes or anything to indicate he was leaving. She walked into the house. Everything was quiet. She went down the hallway to their bedroom and saw that Joe was in bed—she knew something was wrong. It was obvious that he was sleeping, so Randy quietly sat on the bed, trying not to disturb him. She touched his cheek, to see if he had a fever. His eyes opened.

"What's wrong?" she asked softly.

Joe shook his head. "Nothin'," he replied. "Just a little bit sore, and a lot too old to stay up half the night."

Randy looked contrite. "I'm sorry," she said quietly, not meeting his eyes.

Joe said nothing. He had closed his eyes again and shifted his body, as if trying to get comfortable. That was when Randy noticed the dark bruises on his ribs.

"Joe!" she exclaimed, reaching out to touch the bruises. He jumped a little at her touch and promptly reached out to push her hand away.

"Don't, okay?" he said irritably.

Randy was surprised by his anger. "I said I was sorry. Jesus!" she said, his rejection making her speak more harshly than she had meant to. "What else do you want from me?"

Joe opened his eyes again. "I didn't realize that I was asking so much from you," he said. There was no apology in his tone.

"Well, you are." Randy knew she was just responding to his anger, and that she really didn't mean what she was saying. She stood up and left the room.

As she walked into the kitchen the phone rang. She picked it up.

"Hello?"

"Randy?" It was Sarah.

"Hi," Randy said dejectedly.

"Whoa, who died?"

"Just my marriage," Randy replied, sighing.

"What's going on?"

"Joe's mad about last night."

"What's his problem? Hasn't he ever stayed out late, having a good time with the boys?"

"Not really," Randy said, thinking about it. "He mostly stays out late when he goes on search warrants, which was why I thought he'd be gone later last night. Of course, I didn't expect to stay out so late either."

"We were celebrating!" Sarah said. "Or doesn't hubby do that either?" It was clear she didn't think much of Joe's attitude.

Randy laughed. "Yeah, he does do that."

"And isn't he the one with that blonde for a partner?" Sarah asked, her voice indicating her jealousy of Midnight's looks.

"Yeah," Randy said slowly. She knew what Sarah was getting at, but wasn't willing to help her get there.

"So doesn't it bug you just a little bit, that he can be with her all the time but he expects you to stay home and be good?"

"It's not like that."

"Like hell it's not!" Sarah said knowingly.

"Sarah!"

"Come on, Randy. Didn't you tell me he'd done the nasty with her a number of times?"

"Yeah, but—"

"But nothin', babe! Men are pigs, trust me on this. You give that sonofabitch far too much credit. There's a great phrase that describes the difference between men and women, Randy. 'Women need a reason to have sex, men just need a place.' And believe you me, I've been around enough cops to know that that goes double for them!"

"Joe's not like that," Randy said, but she didn't sound so sure. She had always believed Joe was faithful, but Sarah's words seemed to eat away at that conviction.

"Uh-huh," Sarah taunted. "That's what they all say, till they find out the truth. I just don't want you to be one of those broads who says, 'I had no idea this could happen to me.' Believe it, sister, it happens all the time! Besides," Sarah added in for good measure, "I've seen your husband, and let me tell you, he's got 'em lining up. Don't be stupid."

Randy was quiet, thinking about her conversation with Midnight that afternoon, wondering what had prompted Midnight to be so candid about her feelings for Joe and remembering her own thoughts on the depth of their feelings for each other. And now Rick and Midnight were splitting up, and Joe was always the first person Midnight called...

Doubt can be an insidious emotion when paired with uncertainty. Randy spent the rest of the evening wrestling with her thoughts. Many times she tried to tell herself that nothing was going on between Joe and Midnight, and that she was just being crazy. But then she wondered how Midnight could be so casual about a divorce if she didn't already have something else going on. Randy couldn't imagine anyone else Midnight could be involved with than Joe. Hadn't Midnight basically told her that she should go to the academy no matter what Joe said? Maybe she was trying to assure a break up between Joe and her, so that she and Joe could be together. And maybe Joe's current attitude wasn't all about Randy.

By the time Joe got up later that evening, Randy was in a real state of insecurity. She was sitting on the couch, and looked up when Joe walked into the room.

"What's going on with Midnight?" she asked, the question tumbling from her mouth before she could stop it.

"Got me," Joe responded, not sure what she was talking about and wondering if Midnight had called while he slept. He walked over to his jacket, which was lying on the back of an armchair, and pulled out his cell phone. He checked for a message from Midnight. There was nothing.

Randy had watched him as he did this, and when he looked up and asked if Midnight had called, she was sure she saw something guilty in his face.

"No, she didn't call, but maybe you should run right over there and check on her," she retorted.

Joe looked at her as if she'd gone crazy. "What the fuck's wrong with you?" he asked, to Randy's ears sounding every bit like the guilty, cheating husband Sarah had described.

"Oh, there's nothing wrong with me, other than being a naive kid for too long." Randy stood up.

Joe was taken aback by her vehemence, and totally at a loss for a reply. He began to wonder if she'd been drinking—which she had, but not in the quantities Joe was imagining. "I think maybe you need to chill out a little bit, love. You're headin' for a nasty backlash."

In her current state, Randy mistook his words for a threat—that he was telling her not to challenge him or he'd divorce her. She swallowed against the knot that rose in her throat. "Watch me," she said, and left the room.

Joe stood motionless, totally baffled at what had just occurred, not sure what Randy was doing. He all but fell over when she came back out of the hallway with a small suitcase, walked past him, and opened the front door. "I'll get the rest of my stuff later," she said, and walked out.

Joe stared openmouthed at the door after it had closed. He wasn't sure if he should go after her, but remembered that she had been drinking and all but ran out of the house. He caught up to her as she was getting in her car.

"Randy, hold up!" he shouted.

"Just leave me alone, Joe," Randy said, trying to hold back her angry, hurt tears. "You're getting what you want, isn't that good enough for you?" With that she slammed the door and started the engine with a roar. The tires squealed as she slammed the car into reverse and pushed hard on the gas. The last thing she saw was Joe standing in the open doorway to the garage, watching her, shaking his head.

Randy pulled up at Sarah's apartment building half an hour later. She walked up the stairs and rang the doorbell. To Randy's surprise, a man answered. He looked to be in his late thirties or early forties, and he had a stocky build with muscular shoulders. He smiled at Randy, his brown eyes warm and friendly.

"Can I help you?" he asked, his voice not as deep as she had expected, judging from his build.

"Yes." Randy wondered belatedly if she had gotten the wrong apartment. "I'm looking for Sarah."

"Randy?" Sarah's voice came from behind the man. "Dick, move!"

The man laughed and moved out of the way.

Sarah smiled at Randy. "What're you doing here?" she asked as she opened the screen door and motioned her inside.

Randy looked at her friend sheepishly. "Well, I kinda left," she said.

"Left?" Sarah echoed, then understanding dawned on her. "You mean you left Joe?" she said, clearly surprised.

"Well, I thought about what you said, and then he was asking if Midnight had called, and well, I just got mad and left." Randy shrugged, still a little surprised at herself.

"See," Sarah said, wagging her finger at Randy. "Didn't I tell ya!"

"You giving advice again?" Dick said, elbowing Sarah.

"Oh, shut up!" Sarah said, laughing. "Oh! Randy." She looked embarrassed. "This is Dick, my big brother. Dick, this is my friend and soon to be fellow academy classmate, Randy."

Dick smiled at Randy, extending his hand to her. She took it and returned the smile.

"So," Dick said, gesturing for Randy to take a seat. "Do I understand this correctly—you actually left Joe Sinclair?"

Randy was shocked, wondering how Dick knew her last name. She also wondered why he had asked the question the way he had, as if he knew Joe. "I'm sorry…" she began, looking at Sarah.

"Oh, Randy, Dick's SDPD too, remember. He knows Joe," Sarah supplied.

"Oh," Randy said. "That's right, I remember you telling me that you had a brother on the force. I just thought…" She trailed off again before she could put her foot in her mouth about his obvious age. Sarah was only twenty-five.

Sarah laughed, catching Randy's train of thought. "Yes, I am definitely the baby!" She poked her brother in the ribs. "Dick's an ancient forty-one years old!"

"Hey!" Dick said, pretending to be offended.

"Dick's a sergeant with vice," Sarah told Randy.

"Sarah tells me that you two are going to the academy," Dick said.

"Yes." Randy grimaced. "That seems to be part of the problem."

"So Sinclair doesn't want you to be a cop?" Dick looked surprised.

Randy shook her head.

"Hmm." Dick still seemed perplexed.

"What?" Randy asked, bolder than she would normally have been with a man she didn't know.

"If it were me," Dick said, "I'd want my wife to be a cop too. That way she'd understand the ins and outs better. What's Sinclair's beef?"

Randy hesitated, not sure she should discuss Joe's personal tragedies with a total stranger. But he was Sarah's brother, after all. "Well, Joe's kind of overprotective of me, probably because of his parents."

"His parents?" Dick echoed disbelievingly. "What's his parents got to do with you? I mean, were they twisted or something?" His voice had taken on a derisive tone. "From what I heard they were filthy rich and left all that money to him." He looked at Sarah and said melodramatically, "I heard that Scotland Yard even investigated old money bags himself, thinking that he killed them off." He and Sarah laughed, and Randy found herself joining in, even though she really didn't find the information funny. She knew all about what had happened to Joe's parents, and how deeply it had affected him, but she didn't feel that she should try to defend him at this point. It was obvious that Dick Dickerson had his own opinions of Joe, and she didn't want to be rude to someone she had just met. He was, after all, Sarah's brother.

****

172

The next day, Midnight was shocked to find Randy's letter of resignation on her desk. It stated that she was resigning effective immediately. Midnight went to speak to Joe about it, and as soon as she saw him, she knew something major had happened. She walked into his office and shut the door quietly. Joe looked up as he heard it click. Midnight noted that he looked like hell. His blue eyes were bloodshot, and it was obvious he was hungover.

"If it was that bad, why didn't you stay home?" Midnight said, with just enough humor to let him know she was waiting for him to tell her what had happened. Midnight held up Randy's letter. "Does this have anything to do with your mood?"

Joe looked at her blankly, not able to fathom what that piece of paper could have to do with Randy leaving.

"Obviously not," Midnight answered for herself. She looked at him for a moment, gauging what she should tell him. Finally she said, "This is Randy's letter of resignation." She paused. "It's official as of today. Want to explain that to me?"

Joe shook his head slowly, as if trying to catch up. He had no idea that Randy had resigned. "I don't have the faintest notion," he said eventually.

"Great, that's a big help. What did you do this time?" she said, still humorously. All joking went out the window when Joe looked at her—his eyes were deathly serious.

"Night, she left." The words fell like lead weights. Midnight just stared at Joe, shocked into silence. Joe stood up, his anger and confusion driving him to his feet. He strode over to the far wall, then turned around to look at his partner of close to ten years. All he could ask was, "Why?"

The question hung heavily, but Midnight couldn't think of anything to say. She knew what Randy's leaving meant—she knew that Randy had made her decision—but she didn't understand why Randy hadn't waited to see what Joe would do. Then again, maybe she had. "Joe," she began, choosing her words carefully—she knew he was already hurting, and she didn't want to add to that. "What happened before she left? What did she say?"

Joe shook his head as he replayed their last conversation in his mind. He'd spent the whole night drinking and doing the exact same thing. He still hadn't come up with an answer. "I was sleeping when she got home. She came in and we had a few words, but nothing major." He paused, thinking. "When I got up a few hours later, she jumped on me about what was going on with you. I asked if you had called—I thought maybe you'd had another run in with Rick or something. She got real pissed about that... For the life of me, I don't know why. I figured she'd been drinking—she looked it—so I warned her about the monster hangover she was headed for. She jumped up, got some of her things, and left." He was shaking his head again, as if denying to himself that she'd actually gone would make it less real. "That's it."

Midnight had listened to the whole thing, and couldn't put it together either. She knew Randy had been upset about what Midnight had told her the day before, but she didn't see how that related to what Joe was saying had happened. She told him about the conversation between her and Randy, even what she had said about losing him. Joe nodded sadly when she said she'd had to give him up too, but he told her he couldn't see what that had to do with Randy leaving. Obviously, they were missing a few pieces of the puzzle. What bothered Midnight was that they weren't likely to get those pieces if Randy wasn't willing to talk. Both she and Joe were at a loss.

"What are we?" Midnight asked, bewildered and forlorn. "Defective, or something? We can hold together the biggest bunch of misfits and rebels, but we can't seem to hold on to our relationships."

Joe looked at her for a long moment, nodding in agreement. "Maybe we should just stick to what we know," he added, and Midnight agreed.

****

Later that week, Midnight received a phone call from Griff. She hadn't heard from him since the night he brought her home.

"How are you?" he asked, concern tingeing his voice.

"I'm still alive," Midnight answered drily.

"Good to know," Griff said humorously. "Look, believe it or not, this is a business phone call."

"Or not," Midnight interjected.

"Funny. Seriously though, I got a call from the Sacramento Police Department chief. He was wondering if you'd be interested in doing some training for them at their academy in Sacramento."

Midnight was silent for a moment, then asked, "How long are we talking?"

"Maybe a week. But they didn't give me much notice."

"How much notice?"

"A week," he said meekly.

"Gimme a break!" Midnight retorted. "Don't these people plan ahead?"

"Obviously not. Look, if you can't do it, you can't do it."

"Well, wait a minute. Did they say it had to be me?"

"Why?"

"Well, maybe I could send Joe. He's having a rough time right now, and it might be good for him to get out of here for a little while."

"What's wrong with you people?" Griff said, unwittingly echoing Midnight's earlier words.

"You tell me, and we'll both know," Midnight said. "Well, whatddya say—should I give Joe the heads-up?"

"I don't see why not. Maybe he could even do a little range work for them—I hear he's the best shot in the department. Their range master had an accident a couple of weeks back, and he's out of commission for at least this academy class. Think you'd be willing to part with Joe for, say, a couple of months?"

Midnight hesitated, her desire to get Joe away from San Diego and her need for her second-in-command at the office warring with each other. "Maybe, with a little bit of telecommuting and a lot of long-distance phone calls."

"Great!" Griff said. "I'll call the chief back. My chief was hoping you'd be able to help out. He's really interested in your unit, and would like to see your expertise utilized."

"I hope that was a quote," Midnight said, laughing.

"You know I don't use big words like 'utilize' and 'expertise' if I don't have to," Griff joked.

"Tell me," Midnight said. "Well, call me when you have the details, okay?"

"Hey, hey. Don't run off so quick. Have you worked things out with shithead?" He was obviously referring to her errant husband.

"No, we're getting a divorce," she stated blandly.

"Whoa!" Griff was unable to contain his surprise. "You don't screw around, do you?"

"Problem is," Midnight said seriously, "he does."

"Ouch!" Griff sounded as if he'd been burned by her words. "Well, then, does that mean your evenings are free to have dinner with old friends?"

"You mean old friends who never call?"

"No, I mean old friends who have a phone phobia, but would really like to take you to dinner sometime."

Midnight laughed, enjoying the banter. "Okay," she acquiesced, "but I have to warn you, I'm real gun shy right now, so don't expect a lot."

"I won't even bring my gun," Griff replied, understanding her meaning fully.

Midnight laughed again. "Call me sometime next week, okay?"

"How about I fax you?" Griff said, grinning at his end.

"Too technical. How about you pick me up at my place at seven thirty on Friday next week?"

"You got it, I'll see you then."

"Okay, bye." Midnight hung up the phone, her spirits a little brighter, then picked it up again to call Joe.

"Academy training?" he repeated after she had explained the idea, not sure he had heard her right. "In Sacramento?"

"Yes, in Sacramento," Midnight said.

"Isn't it cold up there?"

"Wear a coat."

"Great," he replied. But he knew she was right. He needed to get away for a while, so he could avoid going stir-crazy alone in his house, without his wife.

****

A week later, Joe stayed at home, planning on a raid that evening. He was lying on the couch when Randy walked in. It was obvious she hadn't expected him to be there. Joe sat up slowly, watching her warily.

"I just came to get some of my stuff," Randy said, trying to sound casual. In truth she was a little bit affected by him. She hadn't seen him for a week, and the sight of him now made her realize that she missed him. As if to make things worse, Joe was wearing his favorite faded jeans, and had removed his shirt due to the unseasonably warm, humid weather. Randy had never thought of herself as being attracted to a man's physique, but her heart fluttered a bit at the sight of her husband's bare chest.

"Okay," Joe said, obviously wanting to say more. He still didn't understand what had made her mad enough to leave.

He, in turn, was affected by Randy's unexpected appearance. He reflected that she looked good, dressed much more casually than was her usual style. She was wearing faded jeans that were threadbare at the knees, white canvas shoes, and a turquoise tank top. Her hair was pulled back in a very loose ponytail, and she wore just enough makeup to make her eyes seem to glow.

Randy moved toward their bedroom, wanting to get away from Joe's presence. To her dismay he followed, wanting the exact opposite. He sat casually on the bed with one leg out in front of him, the other stretched down to the floor. Against the cream bedspread, his tan seemed to make him gleam. Randy tried to keep her eyes off of him. She went into their walk-in closet and pulled a suitcase out of one corner, trying to figure out where she could set it in the closet without it being in her way. Finally she decided she didn't have a choice—she had to take it out into the bedroom.

Steeling herself, she walked out and, trying not to look at Joe, who was watching her from the second she reappeared, set the suitcase on the settee in front of the bed. She proceeded to walk back and forth from the closet, finding things she needed. She had been borrowing clothes from Sarah, and had had to buy some pants since Sarah was a size nine and she was only a five. When she was done, having taken very few items that Joe had bought her, she went to get some things from the bathroom. She was relieved to be out of his line of site for a moment. Right up until Joe walked in and stood leaning against the doorjamb.

"Are you planning to speak to me ever again?" he asked lightly.

Randy shrugged, glancing up at him. "Not much left to say, is there?"

"I'd say there's a lot left to say." Joe moved to stand right behind her, staring over her head at her eyes in the mirror.

Randy tensed immediately, but Joe didn't take it as an aggressive movement, more a nervous one. He knew his wife well, even if she wished that he didn't. He raised his hands, placing them on her shoulders. Randy watched him in the mirror; she looked almost afraid. She reminded him of the young, naive woman she had been when they met. Without a word he pulled her back against him. The sensation made Randy's breath come faster. She hadn't realized how much she'd missed his touch until that moment.

She knew, when she looked at Joe, that he was feeling the same thing. His eyes were closed, as if he was trying to memorize the feel of her. The idea of Joe wanting her as much as she did him only served to send another jolt of electricity through her body. Wanting to hold on to this moment, Randy closed her eyes as well, allowing her full weight to lean against him.

She felt Joe's hand move to her hair, pulling the ponytail holder out, allowing her hair to fall against his chest. He buried his hands in it, grasping the golden strands and using them to pull her head back far enough for his lips to meet hers. Randy's self-control left her as she returned his ardent kisses with equal passion. She felt his hands at her waist, and he turned her around to face him, his lips never leaving hers. He lifted her easily and set her on the counter, their lips never losing contact.

Randy reached her hands up, entwining them in his hair and pulling him even closer, eventually encircling his waist with her legs. Joe pulled her tank top from the waist of her jeans. Randy moaned as his hands touched the bare skin of her back, and she tightened her hold on his waist. She touched his bare chest, her nails sliding down to his waist, then to his back. Randy was satisfied to feel him shudder in response.

Joe lifted her, and with her legs still around his waist he carried her to the bed and sat down with her on his lap. He moved his lips to her neck, still caressing her back. When his hands made their way to her breasts, Randy gave up any hope of resisting him. Using her slight weight, she pushed him back on the bed and, watching him as he watched her, she removed her shirt. Then she kissed him again. Time was lost to them as they made love born of passion and longing.

The shadows were lengthening as Joe and Randy lay together on the bed. They were both exhausted, but fulfilled. Joe resisted the urge to ask her the questions that burned in his mind, not wanting to spoil their companionable silence. It occurred to him that he needed to start thinking about getting ready for the raid planned that night. He glanced at the clock. It was 4:30; he had told Midnight he'd meet her at the office at 6:00.

"Shit," he said, the word slipping out before he could stop it.

"What?" Randy asked, sounding tired, but with just a hint of irritation. Joe was amazed at the change in her. She had rarely been irritated with him in the over three years they'd been married, and all of a sudden she seemed annoyed more often than not.

When Joe didn't respond, she sat up and looked at him. Understanding dawned on her. "You have somewhere to be." It was more of a statement than a question.

Joe looked at her for a moment, then nodded. Randy started to move off the bed. Joe reached out, grabbing her hand. "Randy," he started, but she turned on him.

"It's fine, Joe," she said, pulling her hand from his grasp. She reached for her clothes and began putting them on. "You have somewhere to be, and so do I." Her voice was cold and businesslike. Joe didn't like it.

"Oh, Christ, we're back to that, are we?" he asked, angry now too.

"Back to what, Joe?" Randy turned on him, her eyes narrowed. "Back to me packing my things? Well, I guess you could say we are."

"So that's it?" Joe said, incredulous and angry at the same time. "Now you can just make love with me and then walk out?"

"Well, you certainly seem capable of it," Randy shot back. At his stunned expression, she said, "It's just physical, Joe. You should know all about that." She walked into the bathroom, trying desperately not to think of what had happened there only a couple of hours before. Randy was fighting to keep the tears from her eyes. She knew she had been weak in letting herself get carried away with him, and she hated herself for it. "I'll take the stuff I have packed and come get the rest later," she said, managing to keep her voice level.

"Fine," Joe said tonelessly. "I'm leaving town next week for a couple of months. You'll have plenty of time then." His voice didn't express the emotions that were screaming at him to take her in his arms and make her stay. Randy had no idea.

"Two months?" she repeated as she walked back into the room, the smile on her face as wintery as her words. "I'm surprised Midnight would let you go for so long. What ever will she do without you?"

Joe had his jeans on and was buttoning his shirt, but he turned to look at her, his face indicating his confusion. "What the fuck does Midnight have to do with this?"

Randy shrugged. "I just thought she'd need you to run to every time her and Rick have a fight. I mean, who'll hold her hand or do any other service she requires while you're gone?"

Joe was sitting on the bed, pulling on his boots. "What the hell do you have against Midnight now?" he all but yelled.

"Well, nothing, if you don't consider the fact that while she's running her husband off, she's running to mine every other day, crying on his shoulder, needing him, needing God knows what else!"

Joe had to swallow the urge to slap her. "I don't know what's gotten into you lately, but whatever you're on, you better get off it before it eats you alive." He grabbed his jacket off the back of the armchair, picked up his holstered gun, and walked out, slamming the door behind him.

That night, during the raid, Joe was particularly brutal with a gang member who made the mistake of taking a swing at him. Midnight questioned him about the incident later.

"What's gotten into you?" she asked.

Joe shook his head. "I was just pissed and he swung at me. I swung back." He shrugged, downplaying the incident.

"Knocked him clean out is more like it," Midnight joked, but Joe didn't even smile. "Okay, spill it." Midnight knew something was way wrong.

Joe sighed, leaning back in his chair. They were doing the follow-up paperwork on the busts. "Randy came to the house today."

"Yeah?" Midnight prompted when he didn't continue.

"I don't know what to think anymore," Joe said, rubbing his eyes. "One minute she's cold as ice, the next we're making love, and right after that she was back to making nasty comments and being an out and out bitch."

Midnight held up a hand. "Back up! You two, uh…"

"Yeah, don't start with me," Joe said, looking at her darkly when he saw her start to smile.

"I wasn't, I was just surprised. I mean—"

"Yeah, I was surprised myself, but she turned again just as fast."

"Turned how?" Midnight was getting the idea that he was avoiding specifics for a reason.

"She was just being a bitch, Night. It's not her—I don't know what's goin' on with her."

Midnight told Griff about it a couple of days later, on their date.

"So what do you think Randy was doing?" Griff asked, used to the fact that Midnight and Joe were very close and that what affected one of them affected them both.

"I don't know," Midnight said, shaking her head. "I'm beginning to wonder what Randy's real reason for leaving is."

"What did she say?"

"Well, that's the thing—she really didn't. Joe said she wasn't making a lot of sense when she walked out on him. But he said she got really pissed when he asked if I'd called…" She trailed off as she thought about that.

"And?"

"And," Midnight said, sighing, "and… I don't know. We thought she left because she was pissed about him not wanting her to be a cop, but now I just don't know."

They spent the rest of dinner trying to talk about other things, but Griff could see she was still too caught up in her partner's problems. So on the drive home, he asked her about Rick. She got very quiet. He knew he'd run into another roadblock.

Once at her front door, he tilted her chin up to get her to look at him. He searched her blue eyes. "Are you okay?" he asked, knowing that she was under a lot of stress but sensing that something else had happened with Rick.

Midnight nodded, not willing to explain everything that was going on. Rick had been hassling her about some visitation time with Mikeyla and had just been generally difficult at the office, and she was tired of it. And here Joe was getting ready to leave for Sacramento, and she had realized that his being gone was going to be very difficult. "I'm as okay as I can be right now," she said, then reached up and kissed him on the cheek. "Thanks for dinner, Griff. I'm sorry I'm such lousy company right now."

"Nonsense!" Griff said, grinning. "I'll call you sometime this week to check on you, okay?"

"Oh, sure you will," Midnight chided. Griff laughed, then leaned down to kiss her on the forehead. He turned and walked back to his car. Midnight went inside, and after checking on Mikeyla, went to bed. She spent the next few hours tossing and turning, wanting to call Joe, but aware she would have to get used to him not being only a moment away for the next two months.

CHAPTER 9

Jessica Harland smoothed back her deep auburn hair as she waited patiently for Sergeant Sinclair's plane to arrive. She checked the arrivals screen once again to be sure that the plane was still on time. Walking up the stairs to the gates, she pretended not to notice the looks she received. *It's the uniform*, she thought. Her Sacramento Police Department uniform, a color called PD blue—an official-sounding name for dark blue—with the seven-pointed silver star pinned over her heart did tend to make her stand out. With her emerald-green eyes, she was striking, but she never really bothered to accentuate her looks.

She'd grown up in a family of men; her mother had taken care of all of them. Her father had been a cop, her brothers—all three older than her—were cops or detectives, and now she was a cop too. It had been a long, hard battle, harder than she'd expected. There had been many times when she wanted to quit, when her arms were aching from the pushups or her wrists were bruised from the hand-to-hand combat training as well as the handcuffing practice. But she hadn't quit, and her graduation two full months before had been an event in her household. Her mother had been proud of her, although she hadn't really understood why her only girl wanted to get into "the family business." Her father had just about busted a gut when she dropped the bomb that she was using her associate's degree in general education to get into the Sacramento Police Department, and that she was going to the next academy. Her father had had other plans for her; he had sent her to college to become a doctor, or a teacher. But Jessica had her own ideas, and she thought she could do just as good a job as a cop as her brothers.

Jessica had gotten the "peach" of a job of being an assistant at the training academy after, in her first month on the street, she managed to get into a gun fight with some gang members in south Sacramento's seedy area. She'd been terrified, and had been unable to go back to the street right away, not able to qualify at the range because the sounds of gunfire set her nerves on edge. Her father, who was a lieutenant with the department, had assured her that she'd get her nerve back, but Jessica wasn't so sure. She'd been happy to get a chance to "ease back in" by working at the academy with the range master's crew. The month before, the usual range master, Bud Neely, had gone skiing and had managed to fall and break his wrist as well as two fingers on the opposite hand. He was out of the academy training for that class anyway. So the chief had pulled some strings to get not only a replacement range master but a gang expert as well. Jessica had been tasked with picking up the replacement at the airport and driving him out to the Sacramento Police Academy at Yuba College.

She sat at the gate and waited for the plane to arrive. When it did, she stood, looking out for Sergeant Sinclair. She had been told he would be wearing a FORS jacket, which had been described to her, and that he was tall and blond. She began to wonder if he'd missed the flight as the flow of passengers deplaning slowed to a trickle and she still had not seen him. Just when she was about to ask the airline attendant about another incoming flight from San Diego, a man that had to be Sergeant Joseph Sinclair walked up the gangway.

Jessica's first impression of Joe was how light blue his eyes were. When she called out to him, he looked around, his gaze coming to rest on her. For a few moments, Jessica couldn't speak. She just stared up at him and smiled.

"Hi," she said, sounding even to herself like a girl of fourteen. "I'm Jessica Harland. I'll be your assistant on the range."

"Assistant?" Joe asked, his English accent clear. "Why?"

"Well," she said, not sure how to answer, "because they assigned me to you, and I need the paycheck."

Joe grinned at her in spite of himself. She was cute, he thought, almost like Randy had been not too many years ago. He guessed she was probably just about the age Randy had been when he met her.

"If you'll follow me, Sergeant, I'll help you get your bags, and then we can be on our way."

Joe followed her, and when they were standing at the baggage carousel, he took the opportunity to look around at the airport terminal. Not much to see—the terminal was tiny compared to San Diego airport. Then he looked outside, watching the vehicles pull in and away from the curb. Still not much to look at.

"Sacramento's airport is a bit small, isn't it?" Jessica said, as if reading his thoughts.

"That's a pretty safe statement," Joe replied.

"I've never been to San Diego, but I'll bet your airport's a lot bigger."

"A lot," Joe said, watching the carousel for the one bag he'd brought. When the black leather garment bag came around, he grabbed it and turned to Jessica.

"That's it?" she asked, surprised.

"Versus what?"

She shook her head and motioned for him to follow her. As they walked out of the terminal, Joe realized it wasn't as cold as he had expected. Again, Jessica seemed to read his mind.

"We've been having an unseasonably warm spell. Guess it's going to be an early spring this year," she said, stopping next to a black SS Monte Carlo. "Well, this is us." She pulled out the keys and opened the trunk for him.

Joe put his bag inside and removed his FORS jacket, taking a cellular phone out of the pocket before laying the jacket in the trunk as well. He was wearing black jeans, a long-sleeved denim work shirt, and black boots. Jessica noticed the fairly lethal looking gun he wore at his hip, as well as his gold sergeant's shield.

Jessica closed the trunk and explained that the car was actually the property of the Bureau of Narcotic Enforcement. They had sent it over for him, not wanting him to have to spend money on a rental car.

"It's got a full agent compliment," she said, walking over to the passenger's side and beckoning him to follow. She pointed to the dashboard. "You've got your wigwags, as part of the headlight package, and then there's a red light to be utilized if you happen to make a stop. There's also a radio installed, and it's programmed for the PD and the sheriff's office as well as BNE's frequencies. So you should be all set."

She straightened back up. He had nodded to everything she said, and now he was standing next to her, waiting—for what, she wasn't sure.

"Keys?" he said finally.

"Oh!" she replied, a little embarrassed. "I was going to drive you out to the college. It's kind of confusing, and I thought it would give you a chance to adjust to Sacramento…" She trailed off as he shook his head.

"Being a passenger makes me nervous."

"But—"

"I'll drive, you direct."

After a few moments, Jessica shrugged and handed him the keys. Joe promptly unlocked and opened the passenger's door for her. Jessica was taken aback by the gentlemanly gesture; she had started to wonder if he had a problem with women, and maybe that was the reason he didn't want her to drive.

Joe got in the car, putting the keys in the ignition but not starting the engine. He sat looking at the instrument panel, checking out where things were placed. He was used to his Porsche and not really comfortable in a different vehicle. He turned on the police radio, listening to the transmissions and flipping the channels around until he settled on the PD's frequencies; he was most comfortable with their codes and slang. He started the car and turned on the car radio, tuning in a classic rock station. After he'd adjusted the mirrors and his seat, he looked at Jessica, who had watched everything with an amused smile. She wasn't used to such thoroughness.

"Which way?" he asked, grinning.

"Out the gates, and on Five headed south."

Joe nodded, putting the car into gear and easing out of the parking space. Once out of the airport gates, he headed over the bridge to the freeway on-ramp.

"I have to warn you," Jessica said as he turned onto the ramp, "drivers here are more aggressive than you might expect. Your best bet would be to…" She trailed off as Joe accelerated, moving with confidence born of dealing with some of the world's most aggressive drivers. Jessica cleared her throat as Joe began to grin, his eyes still on the road. "Guess you don't need any driving lessons, huh?" she said, her voice belying her embarrassment.

"Guess not," Joe replied. He drove with his left hand, his right hand resting on the gear shift. The sun made the gold on his left ring finger wink—it was then that Jessica noticed the wedding band. She was surprised to feel a stab of disappointment, and knew she wouldn't be the only one.

After directing him to the freeway interchange that would take them toward Marysville, she sat back for the ride. It was a long, boring drive; she'd made it often enough. She still wasn't sure why the department found it necessary to hold its academies all the way out at Yuba College, which was a good forty miles from the PD headquarters.

"So," Joe said, glancing over at her, "you've been a police officer for how long?"

"Two months," Jessica replied.

Joe raised an eyebrow. "And you're how old, if you don't mind me asking?"

"I turned twenty-one three months ago."

Joe nodded. "'Bout what I figured."

"Oh really," Jessica said, smiling. She knew he was kidding her. "And you, Sergeant Sinclair, how long have you been a police officer?"

"A hell of a lot longer than you, I can say that."

"How long?" Jessica asked, not letting him avoid the question that easily.

"Just a bit over ten years," he said, noting the surprised look on her face.

"And you joined the department when you were thirteen?"

"Yeah, right." Joe grinned. He liked her—she was smart, but had an apparent sense of humor too. "More like twenty-three."

Jessica opened her eyes wide. "But that would make you..."

"Way too old!" Joe finished her sentence, remembering a similar conversation with Randy so long ago.

"Well," Jessica said, "if it's any consolation, my father's older than you."

Joe made a choking sound, and then coughed as he began to laugh. "Thanks!" They laughed, comfortable with each other already.

"So, what made you get into gang work?" she asked.

"Probably being in one," Joe replied. He could tell he'd surprised her again.

"You were in a gang?"

"The leader of one, actually."

"Really?" She watched him nod. "And your accent—it's English, isn't it?" Again Joe nodded. "They have gangs in England?"

Joe rolled his eyes at her, having heard the question a few times before. "Why does everybody ask that?"

"Well, England conjures up pictures of kings and queens, the Beatles, castles, and knights, not gangs."

"Well, we have the other stuff too, but yes, there are gangs in England."

"What part of England are you from?"

"London."

"I just can't picture you as a poor kid of the rough-and-tumble London streets."

"Well, picture London society and a mansion on a hundred and twenty acres, and you'd be closer to the truth," Joe replied, shocking her into silence this time.

"You were a rich kid?" she finally managed, sure he was kidding.

"Was, am, yeah." He wasn't sure why he was telling her this.

"You're rich?" she said skeptically. "No way!"

Joe nodded, but Jessica continued to look at him disbelievingly. "I don't believe it," she said.

"What do ya want, a bank statement?" Joe said, his smile broad. Just then his cell rang. He unclipped it from his belt and looked at the number, grinning. "That didn't take long," he said to himself.

"What?" Jessica asked, just as he answered. There was a wide grin on his face as the person on the other end spoke.

"What?" he said. He sounded exasperated, but was smiling all the while. Jessica watched as he listened, then began to laugh.

"Well, that took, what"—he looked at his watch—"all of about two hours." He listened for a moment. "Look, I did that warrant myself—don't let Rick screw it up. You know he's just broodin' about you—make him run it." He shook his head. "No, it should be just the way I laid it out, he's just makin' excuses." He was quiet for another moment, glancing over at Jessica and rolling his eyes. "Look, if he wants to fight about it, you have him call me. Otherwise, tell the dumb sonofabitch that if he doesn't do it my way I'm gonna call his mum and tell her he's being a spoiled brat again." He laughed in response to what the other person was saying. Jessica watched, fascinated by his obvious ease with whoever he was talking to. He looked over at her and winked.

"Hey, Night," he said into the phone. "I need ya to do something for me. Tell this police officer about my financial situation."

"What?" Midnight asked, confused now.

"Just do it, hold on." He handed the phone to Jessica. Jessica stared at it for a moment, then looked at Joe; he nodded to her. "Go ahead, it's my boss."

Finally she took the phone. "Hello?"

"Hi, who're you?" Midnight asked, her voice light.

"Me? Oh, I'm Officer Jessica Harland of the Sacramento Police Department."

"And how did you get stuck with my partner?"

"I, uh," Jessica stammered, surprised that Joe had a female for a partner. "Well, I was asked to drive Sergeant Sinclair to the training site."

"Are you driving?" Midnight asked, surprised.

"Well, no, ma'am, he is." Jessica was taken aback when the woman on the other end of the line began to laugh.

"Yeah, that's definitely Joe you've got there. He hates to be a passenger, basically has to be unconscious if he's not driving. Anyway, he told me to tell you about his financial situation?"

194

"Well, yes, ma'am. We were having this discussion and he told me something that was rather hard to believe."

"He told you he was rich," Midnight said. It was a statement, not a question.

"Yes, he did, but I didn't believe him."

"Well, I'm Lieutenant Midnight Chevalier, and I'm here to tell you that the man is not lying. He's worth, oh, a few million now, I'd say."

"I…" Jessica hesitated, stunned first by the rank of the woman she was having this outrageous conversation with, and second by the amount the lieutenant had stated. "Yes, ma'am, I believe it now," she finally managed. "Thank you, ma'am." She handed the phone back to Joe, who was laughing by now.

"What'd you tell her?" he asked. "She's gone quite pale now."

"I told her what you wanted me to, Sinclair. Now I've gotta go. Rick's pacing outside my door, and I'm not in the mood to get into another one with him. I'll talk to you later."

"Okay, bye." Joe hung up. Looking at Jessica, he said, "Believe me now?"

She nodded. "Unequivocally." She was silent for a moment, then cocked her head to the side. "Your boss is a female?"

"Yeah," Joe said, shrugging. "So?"

"I just…" Jessica hesitated for a moment "I'm surprised, that's all."

"Why?" Joe asked, his brow furrowing.

"Well, most men don't like to work for women, especially cops."

Joe seemed to consider her statement for a minute, then shrugged again. "Maybe some men, but I wouldn't even consider crossing my partner. She'd probably kill me."

Jessica looked at him, confusion obvious on her face. "Is she your boss or your partner? She said 'partner,' and you've said both."

"Midnight is my boss—she runs FORS—but we're partners too. I'm her second."

"Second?"

"In command."

"Oh." Jessica found herself respecting Joe more for not only having a woman for a boss, but obviously thinking a great deal of her as well. Then something occurred to her. "She's not your wife, is she?"

Again Joe raised an eyebrow at her. "What made you ask that?"

"I'm sorry," Jessica said, thinking she had offended him.

"No, it's okay, I just thought it was an interesting avenue for you to take, and I wondered how you got there."

"Well," Jessica said, still a little hesitant, "I noticed your wedding band earlier, and I also noted how close the two of you seemed to be on the phone, and…" She shook her head. "I'm probably way off base, huh?"

Joe surprised her. "Not really. Her and I are pretty close, but no, she's not my wife. She is the wife of my best friend, for the time being."

"The wife, or the best friend?" Jessica asked, curiosity getting the better of her.

"What?"

"Is she his wife for the time being, or your best friend for the time being? Or both?"

Joe grinned. She did have a quick mind. He looked at her. "Have you ever considered becoming a detective?"

"Actually," Jessica said, smiling proudly, "the thought has occurred to me."

"You'd do pretty well, I'd wager. But yes, she is his wife for the time being—they're getting a divorce. And as for him being my best friend, well, Midnight is too, and he's the one screwing up." He shrugged, indicating that he didn't know what else he could do.

"Pretty tangled web you San Diegans weave down there, isn't it?" Jessica said.

"You haven't even heard my half of it," Joe said. Jessica was about to ask for his half of it when she noticed his face had become really serious, and she decided that if he wanted to tell her, he would. Joe didn't say anything for a while.

"So tell me about this range. What are the facilities like?" he asked eventually. Jessica found herself glad she hadn't asked him about his story, sensing that he didn't want to discuss it. She began telling him about the range and the academy at Yuba College, and the rest of the drive passed quickly.

****

In San Diego, Midnight had to deal with Rick, who was not pleased about having to go through his wife instead of Joe, who was really his boss. Besides the fact that he didn't like the raid layout Joe had set up, he had to deal with Midnight on top of it, and she basically didn't have the patience at the moment to be tactful.

"Look, Rick, you'll do it the way Joe laid it out or you're off the team on this one. I don't have time to hold your hand and explain it to you again."

Rick looked at his wife, narrowing his eyes at her tone. He did not like the way she talked to him as if to a child. "I've been in this unit for almost four years now. I think I know when something is right, and this isn't right, Midnight. Stop being so goddamned hardheaded and listen to me!"

Midnight was shaking her head. "I don't have time for this. If you don't want to lead the team, I'll fucking do it." She picked up the paperwork on his desk and walked out of his area.

"Shit!" Rick jumped up to stride after her, his long legs catching up to her easily as she entered her office.

"What now?" Midnight asked irritably.

She looked tired, and Rick could tell she was really in no shape to do the raid. It irritated him more that he cared about what happened to her. He knew Joe's original raid plan was missing something, but he couldn't convince Midnight that he knew what he was talking about, because he couldn't put his finger on what was making him uncomfortable about the plan.

Midnight was watching him now. She'd turned around, and he'd walked straight up to her, so she had to look up to make eye contact with him.

"Damn it, Night, you know I don't make noise about things unless I have a reason," Rick insisted. Midnight noted that he had shortened her name automatically, as he often did when he was worried about her.

She started to shake her head again. "I just think Joe's right on this one. He knows his stuff when it comes to these guys." She was trying to reason with him but not really getting anywhere.

"Not this time, Night. I can feel it," Rick said, staring down at her.

Midnight sighed. "Well, I'm not changin' his game plan unless you can give me a good reason to, and feelings are not gonna cut it."

Rick searched her face, knowing he was fighting a losing battle but unwilling to let her lead a plan he wasn't comfortable with. "Fine," he said finally, holding up his hands in defeat, "but I'll lead it."

His voice left no room for argument, and Midnight wasn't really in the mood to give him one. She nodded. Rick turned and walked out of the office. She went to her desk and sat down, closing her eyes for a moment. Fighting with him was becoming a tiring task; part of her wished he would transfer. At least if he did, she wouldn't have to worry about him countermanding her all the time.

Two and a half hours later, Kana, one of Midnight's oldest female members, threw open her office door. "Midnight, there's trouble."

Midnight's head snapped up at the tone of Kana's voice. "Where?" she asked, but a cold feeling was already clenching in her stomach, making her want to throw up.

"Rick's crew, they're in trouble. Back up's already on the way."

Midnight jumped up, grabbing her FORS jacket and putting her gun at the small of her back. "Let's go."

Midnight drove her Corvette like a madwoman, blowing lights and stop signs all through the city. Once on the freeway, she did a hundred miles an hour, racing toward the house in east San Diego that Rick and his unit had been set to raid. As she turned onto the street, she saw the police cars and then the ambulances. Pulling right up to the scene, she vaulted out of the car almost before it had come to a complete stop.

She headed for the house at a dead run. A uniformed police officer moved to stop her; with a fluid movement of a booted foot, she dropped him to the lawn.

"I'm a cop, these're my people," she said as she headed for the front door.

Kana was not two steps behind her. When Midnight reached the door she stopped, staring at the havoc around her. She saw two of her people lying on the floor—both were conscious and being tended to by paramedics. Midnight felt a churning in her stomach, and she knew she had to find him. She moved as if in a nightmare through the house, heading for the back—Rick always hit the back door. When she got there, she didn't see him. There were police officers everywhere, but she didn't see Rick. The fear in her stomach continued to grow. She moved through the other rooms, then went up to the second floor. She spotted him lying in the hallway.

"No!" she screamed, running toward him. He didn't move. Midnight slid to a stop on her knees at his side. She reached out to touch his face. It was cool. Brushing aside his curly brown hair, she saw blood and immediately turned and screamed down the hallway, "Get a paramedic up here, now!" She heard her call echoed by Kana, who was standing halfway up the staircase.

"Rick," Midnight said, putting her lips down to his ear. "Come on, you sonofabitch, you can't get out of this divorce this easily. Wake up!" Her voice was harsh and angry, her tears flowing down her face. "Please," she said, a mere whisper. The whole world seemed to be spinning as she held her breath, waiting to hear or see something, anything. "Please," she whispered again, her lips brushing his cheek.

She heard the lowest moan escape his lips, and she expelled her breath, her head pounding from the adrenaline that was pumping through her veins. She sat back as he started to move his head.

"Don't move, babe," she said as he tried to lift his head. "Just wait for the paramedics."

She saw a dark blue eye looking at her from amidst his curls. "Who're you again?" he said, his voice rough as he began coughing.

She automatically reached for him, trying to help him as he struggled to sit up, his knees supporting his arms, which in turn supported his head. Upon closer inspection, she noted that he'd taken a pretty nasty blow to the head, probably from the butt of a gun, but otherwise he seemed okay. As the paramedics came upstairs and took over examining him, Midnight stood, feeling the world spin out of control. She moved toward the stairs, blindly passing Kana, who turned and ushered her down the steps and out the back door. Midnight proceeded to throw up, down on all fours. She sat on the ground and leaned her head against the back stairs she had just vaulted down. Kana was sitting next to her.

"He okay?" Kana asked.

Midnight nodded, closing her eyes in relief.

Kana watched her leader closely. She knew, much like everyone else in FORS, that Rick and Midnight were on the outs, but she also knew Midnight would have moved heaven and earth moments before to get to her husband. Kana knew she'd sell her very soul for a love that deep.

After she recovered from being sick, Midnight stood, brushing off her jeans. She looked at Kana for a long moment. Kana was watching her, as if to make sure Midnight herself was okay. Midnight pulled a grin at the other woman, and Kana began to smile too. She respected this compact blond who was the driving force behind their very successful "gang." Midnight walked up the stairs leading to the back door of the house. Once inside, she went to check on the two injured members she had seen upon first entering. She was told they were out in one of the ambulances. She walked outside, running into the police officer she had taken down on her way in. He was an older man, in his early fifties. As she looked up at him, he inclined his head to her, and she beamed an embarrassed smile at him.

"Sorry about that," she said as she gestured to his uniform pants, still dirty from where he had landed.

The officer looked down, then at her, breaking into a smile of his own. "That's okay. I haven't been tackled by a woman like that in years!" He gave her a two-fingered salute as she walked away, laughing.

Midnight went to the ambulances, showing her badge to the medical personnel. She looked in on her people. Dave Dibbins was one of the injured. He'd taken a round in the shoulder, but he seemed in good spirits. Manny was the other person; he had what looked like a head wound, but he was sitting up, looking around.

"Some party, huh?" Dibbins said, smiling at Midnight.

"Yeah, looks like they had some interesting party favors too," Midnight replied. She looked to the medic to her right. "Are they okay?"

The female paramedic nodded toward Dibbins and said, "He's got a fractured shoulder from the bullet, and that other one's just a graze, but we're gonna keep him overnight for observation."

"Like hell!" Manny said, shaking his head.

"Oh, yes, I think so," Midnight said, smiling at her newest member.

"Only if you'll be my nurse," Manny said, his smile wide.

"What've I told you about that?" came a familiar English accent from behind Midnight. She turned, almost bumping into Rick. He was holding a bandage to the side of his head. Midnight looked up at him, her face reflecting an unspoken apology. "Rick..." she began, but he shook his head slowly.

"Don't," he said quietly. "We're alright." He looked from her to the two men in the ambulance. "Right?"

"Yeah," Dave said, "if you don't count the bullet in my shoulder and Manny's little scratch." He sounded sarcastic, but he was joking.

The female paramedic moved to Rick's side, taking the bandage from him. Midnight moved out of the way, walking over to her car. She was standing in the open driver's door, her head resting on her arms, when Rick came up behind her. She felt his presence before he even spoke.

"Night," he said quietly.

She turned to look at him, the door of the car between them. "I'm sorry," she said, before he could say anything. "You were right, and I should've listened. I just..." She paused, shaking her head in self-reproach. "I was thinking you were just trying to challenge me. It was stupid and I'm sorry. It won't happen again." She was looking right at him as she made her confession.

Rick looked at her for a long moment, recalling an incident between them a long time back, shortly after they'd met, and after they'd had a particularly physical sexual confrontation. The day afterward, Midnight had questioned his ability to handle himself in a fight. Later she had apologized for her unprofessional behavior. He had noted at the time that she was sorry about being unprofessional—unprofessional, yes, but human, *never*. He felt this conversation had the same flavor. She was sorry about doubting his professional opinion, but not his fidelity. Finally, he shook his head, laughing.

"What?" she asked, having no idea of the direction of his thoughts.

"Nothin', Midnight. Let's just say you're nothing if not consistent."

Midnight looked at him, quirking an eyebrow. "Maybe they should check you again. They may have missed more of an injury than they thought."

Rick grinned, and without warning leaned over the car door and kissed her softly on the lips, then moved to whisper in her ear, "It's just nice to know you still care whether I live or die." He walked away, leaving Midnight to stare after him. After a few moments a slow smile crossed her lips. Maybe all wasn't completely lost after all. She'd have to see where his true loyalties lie.

You can find more information about the author and series here:

www.sherrylhancock.com

www.facebook.com/SherrylDHancock

Also by Sherryl D. Hancock:

The *WeHo* series follows a group of women from Los Angeles as they navigate the ups and downs of love, life, work, and everything in between.

www.vulpine-press.com/we-ho

The *Wild Irish Silence* series. Escape into the world of BJ Sparks and discover how he went from the small-town boy to the world-famous rock star.

www.vulpine-press.com/wild-irish-silence-series

www.ingramcontent.com/pod-product-compliance
Lightning Source LLC
Chambersburg PA
CBHW031957170626
46807CB00006B/2521